PRAISE FOR:

The Colors of Home

Finding home isn't always easy after your heart s been broken, but Edwina Perkins shows us the way in this beautiful novel packed with family drama, belonging and forgiveness.

—Vanessa Miller, USA Today Bestselling Author of *The Filling Station*

In *The Colors of Home*, author Edwina Perkins shows both the issues surrounding racism and the victory of growth when we accept one another on the basis of who we are rather than skin color. This book is a realistic look—not at a biracial family, but a family, something we can all identify with. *The Colors of Home* will open your eyes, delight your "reading heart," and bring you to new understandings and hopes for the future of God's worldwide family. This is the novel I've waited years for. Lucky you! You only have to turn a few pages!

—Eva Marie Everson, CEO, Word Weavers International, ECPA Bestselling Author of *Miss Beth Bettencourt*

Edwina Perkins has written an intriguing, must-finish novel; even more impressive is the warmth and tenderness with which she writes the novel.

—Cecil Murphey, author or co-author of 140 books, including the international best sellers *90 Minutes in Heaven* with Don Piper and *Gifted Hands* with Dr. Ben Carson.

The Colors of Home is a brave and tender novel about grief, belonging, and the hard work of reconciliation. With deep compassion and honesty, Edwina Perkins invites us into what it really looks like to keep choosing love even when fear, pain, and injustice whisper that retreat is safer. Ebony McMullen's journey is one of quiet courage—fighting for her family, her faith, and the hope that healing is still possible. This is a story that reminds us God often does His most transformative work in our broken places, and that home isn't always where we start, sometimes it's what we build together, one faithful, faltering, grace-filled step at a time.

—Edie Melson, Director of the Blue Ridge Mountains Christian Writers Conference, Author of *Soul Care When You're Weary*

The Colors of Home is a tender, unflinching story of grief, love, and resilience. Edwina Perkins writes with rare honesty and compassion, inviting readers into the intimate journey of a mother navigating loss while fiercely holding her family together. Every page pulse with emotion, faith, and humanity, reminding us that "home" is not just a place, but the people, memories, and hope we carry forward. This novel does not rush healing; it honors it. A deeply moving and beautifully written story that stays with you long after the final page.

—Dr. Kennita "Dr. Kay" Williams, Author, Leadership & Wellness Advocate

The Colors of Home invites you to journey alongside a family navigating lives that didn't unfold the way they expected and situations they never would have chosen. Sound familiar? That's because this is real life—beautifully messy and achingly authentic.

The characters are richly drawn, and you'll find yourself turning pages late into the night, eager to discover how each one faces the obstacles before them. If you're trying to live well in a world that can be complicated and unpredictable, this book is for you. It's a story that reminds us we're not alone in the mess, and that grace meets us right where we are.

—Margot Starbuck, Author of *Small Things With Great Love*

Edwina Perkins' book tackles tough realities, even within the church, while offering hope and reconciliation as a small community changes hearts one person at a time. She presents an everyday story where unspoken stigmas are woven subtly throughout—cycles of hurt, prejudice, and the ways people dehumanize one another—unfolding as naturally as a movie you can't look away from. Through the rippling waves of everyday life and crisis of faith, *The Colors of Home* beautifully unravels the moving hand of God on hearts, making all things beautiful in time.

—Dr. Karynthia Glasper Phillips, Author of *Press Pause: Making Time for God in an Overscheduled Life*

The Colors of Home

Edwina Perkins

The Colors of Home, Edwina Perkins
Issued in electronic and paperback formats.
Paperback ISBN: 978-1-970354-17-1
E-book ISBN: 978-1-970354-18-8
LCCN: 2026907264

First Edition

Publisher: Dressed in Love Press, LLC
www.drkatherinehayes.com

Cover Designer: Katherine Hutchinson-Hayes
Book Interior Designer: Jenifer Jennings

Printed in the United States of America

For Cec, my biggest fan

Sydney, my biggest cheerleader

David, my biggest advocate

And everyone who packs up their pain and moves toward hope,

trusting God with the unpacking.

Table of Contents

Welcome to
Home
DINER
Shane's
HARDWARE
Elementary
School
MORNING GLORY RD
Ebony's House

Chapter 1

"Mail's here!" Destiny sang from the hallway, dragging the word out like a colorful ribbon. She appeared in the doorway of the living room, clutching three envelopes to her small chest, her pajama top inside out, her braids frizzy and crooked, the way things had been since grief rearranged all the little routines. Ebony stopped hearing the mail the day her husband died. The scrape of the slot. The hollow *thunk* of envelopes striking hardwood. The small, daily announcement that the world was still moving, delivering, demanding. Once, the sound had been as familiar as a heartbeat, her house clearing its throat every afternoon. Today, she only noticed the mail because her daughter did.

Destiny studied her mother's face, her almond-slanted eyes narrowing slightly. "You, sad, Mama?"

"I'm okay," Ebony lied.

The child lingered a moment, reading her mother's expression, then looked away as if she already sensed what kind of day it would be before anyone had to say a word.

"Thank you for getting the mail, Princess." Ebony forced a smile that didn't reach her cheeks. "Let's see what you got today."

Destiny crossed the room and placed the stack on the coffee table in front of Ebony with gentle hands, the same tenderness she showed to everything that mattered, especially ladybugs. She moved through the world cautiously, careful not to crush what others didn't even see.

Destiny patted the top envelope and whispered, as if she were giving the mail secret instructions. "Be nice to my Mama," she said to the letters,

A chair scraped.

Michael? Ebony's head jerked so fast her neck hurt. Nobody was there. *Of course, nobody is there. Of course, Michael's still dead.* Ebony rubbed her temples. Her mind had been drifting again, somewhere between the living and the gone, where memory played tricks and voices slipped through walls. The scrape came from Owen moving a stool back with his foot as he stepped into the living room. He wore the same hoodie he'd worn the day before and the day before that. The hood stayed up more often than not now, as if hiding his face could hold the world back.

"Want me to put some water on for your coffee?" he asked.

"Yes," Ebony said automatically.

Owen's gaze moved to the mail stack, then away. He didn't ask. He acted like questions were a kind of betrayal, as if giving the bad news a name made it true. "You got it," he said and hurried to the kitchen to fill the kettle, then set it on the stove.

Scotty came next, stomping down the hallway like the floor had personally offended him. Sixteen and taller than Ebony, shoulders broad with promise and anger. His hair was still wet. He smelled of the cheap cedar soap Ebony bought because it was on sale.

"Yes?" he snapped, seeing her looking at him.

Ebony blinked. "Nothing."

Scotty's eyes flicked to the mail. "Are those more bills?"

She opened her mouth to answer, but the words stuck. Her throat had become a drawer that jammed whenever she tried to pull out the truth.

Destiny climbed onto the leather couch beside Ebony and leaned her head against her mother's shoulder. The child's breath was soft, her body heavy with trust. Ebony let her cheek rest against Destiny's unkempt hair for half a second longer than necessary. Recently, Ebony felt like she was holding her family together with bubble gum and tape. She sighed and picked up the top envelope. The return address was printed in a font that didn't care about pain. It didn't stutter. It didn't apologize. It didn't soften itself for widows. Final Notice. Ebony's stomach tightened so hard it felt like a fist.

Owen's jaw tensed. He'd seen the letters before.

Scotty leaned closer, eyes narrowing as if he could out-stare the problem into submission.

Ebony slid a finger under the flap. She told herself to breathe, that she was an adult. She knew her husband was dead, and she was still alive, and that meant she had to keep going. The paper inside was crisp. Too crisp for what it contained, like the threat had been ironed. She scanned. Mortgage delinquency, failure to remit, and foreclosure proceedings. Her vision blurred. Not with tears. With something graver. The sudden absence of the future.

SILVER RIDGE FINANCIAL GROUP

Mortgage Servicing Division
1450 Westbrook Plaza
Denver, CO 80202
Phone: (800) 555-1948

LOAN NUMBER: 4478-2219-MC   DATE: October 14, 2024

NOTICE OF DEFAULT AND INTENT TO FORECLOSE

To: Ebony McMullen
      Michael McMullen
      233 Canterberry Lane
      Boulder, CO 80302

Dear Mr. and Mrs. **McMullen,**

This letter serves as formal notification that your mortgage loan secured by the property located at **233 Canterberry Lane, Boulder, Colorado 80302,** is in default due to failure to make required monthly payments.

As of October 1, 2024, the total amount **past due** is **$18,742.36,** which includes missed payments, accrued interest, late fees, and administrative costs.

Unless the **total past-due** amount is received in **certified funds no later than November 18, 2024,** Silver Ridge Financial Group will initiate foreclosure proceedings in accordance with Colorado state law.

You have the right to:

- Reinstate the loan by paying the full amount due
- Request a loan modification review
- Seek housing counseling assistance

To discuss reinstatement options, contact our Loss Mitigation Department at (800) 555-1948 within ten (10) business days of receipt of this notice.

Failure to respond may result in acceleration of the full loan balance and sale of the property at public auction.

This communication is from a **debt** collector. This is an attempt to collect a debt, and any information obtained will be used for that purpose.

Daniel R. Whitaker
Vice President, Mortgage Servicing
Silver Ridge Financial Group

Ebony looked up, realizing she'd gotten up from the couch and had been pacing the floor in front of the fireplace. For a split second, her eyes landed on the framed photo on the mantle where she'd stopped. Her husband.

Michael's grin caught in motion like a living thing. His arm was around Ebony's shoulder. His cheek pressed against hers like he belonged there. He'd been white. Not "sort-of." Not "close enough." White like fresh snow and lightning. White, like the kind of man people looked at and *assumed* was safe.

Ebony had gotten used to the stares when they walked into restaurants together. The quick double-takes at school events. The woman at the grocery store who once asked if Ebony was the nanny. She'd gotten used to it. What she hadn't gotten used to was how quickly "we" became "you" when he died.

Ebony's fingers trembled.

"What does it say?" Scotty asked.

Owen crossed his arms. "C'mon. Stop playing dumb. We already know what it says."

"Owen—" Ebony started.

"It says we're broke," he snapped. "It says you didn't have a plan."

She flinched and resisted the urge to scream.

Scotty walked to his brother, his fists balled. "Don't talk to our Mom like that."

Owen's laugh was sharp. "Why not? Everybody else thinks it. You think the bank cares that Dad is—" His voice broke on the word, as if it had teeth. He tried again, harder, meaner. "That Dad is gone?"

Destiny walked to her mom, her hand tightening around Ebony's forearm. Ebony looked down at the scared expression on Destiny's face, knowing her youngest didn't like fights. "I'm sorry we raised our voices, Princess. Everything's fine," she said, trying to quell the tension Destiny soaked up like a sponge, tension she'd spent thirteen years learning to wring from the world before it soaked into her daughter.

Ebony folded the letter carefully, as if neatness could change it. Like the paper might be less true if it were less messy. She set it down and avoided her children's stares.

From the kitchen came the hiss of the kettle.

Ebony stood too fast, and the floor tilted. She rushed into the kitchen to shut off the burner, and the whistle died. Heaping spoonfuls of instant coffee, sugar, and creamer hit her mug. She stirred the muddy mixture and stared at the faded rectangle where their fancy espresso machine used to sit. Gone. Pawned for groceries, school lunches, and Scotty's new uniform. Stainless steel traded for survival. For weeks, she'd moved through the days like a person underwater. Everything she did was slow, heavy, muffled. She'd made countless calls, filled out the forms, arranged the funeral, ordered the headstone, accepted the condolences, and the casseroles. She'd signed papers that'd stolen the color from her life. She'd tried. Really tried. But trying didn't pay the mortgage.

Ebony took a sip of her steaming coffee and turned to see Owen behind her. Not talking, just… being there. The way he'd started doing since the funeral, as if his presence could hold her upright. He went back and forth between fighting her and protecting her.

"Sorry about what I said. Scotty and I should know better than to raise our voices around Destiny. We'll figure it out," he said quietly. "Sometimes, I don't know what's wrong with me."

She nodded. "We're all trying to get through this the best way we can." Lifting the mug to her lips, Ebony let the bitter heat steady her as she watched her son. Owen's eyes were her husband's eyes in a different face. That same steady green stare, the same calm in the middle of chaos. It made something in Ebony shatter. A hairline fracture of fear and love. "You're eighteen," Ebony whispered, hating how small her voice sounded.

"So?"

"So, you shouldn't have to be—" Ebony stopped herself before she said, 'the man of the house.' Her husband had hated that phrase and said it was a curse people put on boys too early.

"I won't ever be Dad." Owen's gaze shifted for a second. Then he focused back on her eyes. "But I'm here. For us."

Scotty walked into the kitchen. "Aren't we going to talk about our choices?"

Ebony's eyes burned. "We don't have many choices," she said and wiped her face.

"Yes, we do," Scotty said. "We can fight to stay here. Owen and I can get jobs to help out, and I promise there will be—"

"Or we can go where Dad's family is." Ebony cleared her throat and twisted a ringlet around her finger. "Look, I've been thinking about this a lot lately. I've even spoken at length with your Uncle Gabe about it." She straightened her slumped shoulders. "We can go to North Carolina. Your grandfather left his house to his son. It would mean—"

"Don't say his name like it's a solution," Owen said. "He's never liked us."

Ebony's chest tightened. "At least he's alive."

The words hung in the air, ugly and true.

Destiny walked into the kitchen, her eyes wide. She looked from Owen to Ebony. "Don't fight," she said, her voice soft. "We are *togefer*."

Ebony's breath hitched. That was the thing grief tried to steal. Unity. Being together. Ebony returned to the couch, reached out, and pulled Destiny into her arms, holding her close enough to feel her heartbeat.

"What do we really have in North Carolina?" Owen asked, his voice steadier now. "Is it true, Dad's childhood home is ours?"

Ebony nodded, wishing she could avoid the question because it was too complicated to answer truthfully. A racist father-in-law and a house that might not even still be standing awaited them in North Carolina. She had no savings, no miracle on the way, no partner to share the load, no safety net. Just three kids and a long road ahead. "I have a key," she said.

Scotty frowned. "To what?"

Ebony looked past them, out the kitchen window, at the Colorado sky that used to feel like freedom. The mountains in the distance stood there as they'd always stood there, indifferent and gorgeous. "A house," she said. "And a barn."

"Mama, can you hug me?" Destiny asked.

Ebony cradled her mug as she held Destiny's hand and walked back into the adjacent living room to the couch. Destiny snuggled beside her as her stubby fingers stroked her mother's cheek.

The boys sat down across from Ebony in the love seat opposite the oversized couch.

Ebony took another sip of her coffee and closed her eyes, allowing the grief to flow just enough to make the final decision. "We're leaving," she announced as she opened her eyes.

"But it's the middle of the school year," Scotty said. "Who gets up and moves cross-country in October?"

Owen rolled his shoulders back and frowned. "It's true, Mom. It's a weird time to move with two kids to start school in the middle of—"

"This works in our favor." She opened the family Bible on the nearby end table, removing a crumpled piece of paper. She held up the brochure she'd discovered days before in Michael's desk, on what seemed like the millionth time she attempted to clear it out. "I found out that Home has a year-round-schedule."

"Are you kidding me!" Scotty threw his hands into the air. "We're going to a district that has school the entire year. It doesn't get any worse than this."

"Hear me out, kids," Ebony said. "Home's district doesn't add any extra days of school. What it means is they have a schedule with shorter gaps in between. Right now, they're on fall break, and they return to class in a month. This works out great because we'll get there in time to get settled before the new semester."

"We're really leaving?" Owen asked.

"Yes. We're really leaving." Ebony exhaled. "We're going to move to Home." She sat back, allowing relief to flood through her over what she hadn't been able to say since the funeral.

Chapter 2

Ebony

Ebony didn't start packing until she cleaned. It wasn't logical. It wasn't efficient. It wasn't even necessary. But grief made its own rules, and one of Ebony's rules—unspoken, stubborn—was that she couldn't leave this house looking like abandonment. She couldn't let the last place that held her husband's laughter become a pile of boxes and panic. She needed the rooms to look… respectful. Like they'd been loved.

She wiped the kitchen counter twice, even though it was already clean. The sponge moved in slow circles, chasing a spot that wasn't there. The sun coming through the window caught the steam rising from the kettle she'd forgotten about again, and for a moment it looked like breath. She stopped. *Breath.*

The memory came fast and mean: the hospital room, the beep that stopped, the way the nurse's mouth moved like she was speaking underwater, the way Ebony's world went quiet except for the sound of her own pulse banging against her ribs.

"Mom?" Owen's voice pulled her back. He stood in the doorway, shoulders filling the frame. There was something about him that still startled her. How quickly he had become tall, how quickly he had become serious. He was wearing jeans and boots, as if he were ready for work or war. In his hand was a roll of packing tape.

Ebony stared at it too long, as if she'd never seen tape before. "Where'd you get that?" she asked.

Owen lifted a shoulder. "Neighbor. Mr. Cates. He said he had extra."

Ebony smiled in spite of herself. The Cates. Virginia had been baking cookies for this family since Owen was in diapers. Sprinkles cookies for Destiny without being asked. She'd held Ebony through more than one hospital waiting room. Now that chapter was closing too.

"She's bringing some over later," Owen said.

"Of course she is." Ebony would miss them more than she could say.

Owen stepped into the kitchen and set the tape down near the fruit bowl. They hadn't bought fruit in two weeks. She kept forgetting. Or maybe she remembered and just didn't want to feel the cost of fresh things. The bowl held three bruised apples, and an orange that had started to pucker like it was embarrassed. Owen leaned his hip against the counter. "What's the plan?"

"And the house?" Owen asked, too carefully.

Ebony's throat tightened. "The bank gets it."

Owen's eyes flickered, just once, toward the living room. Toward the mantle. Toward the photo.

Ebony didn't look. She was learning that some things, if she looked too long, would rip her open in a way she couldn't put back together.

Footsteps thumped in the hallway. Scotty came in hard, energy sharp. He had on his school hoodie—Homecoming Champions 2024— like the year had been kind, and he wanted to wear proof that life had once been normal. His gaze landed on the tape, then on his mother. "You're really doing it."

Ebony kept folding the towel. "Yes."

"We're leaving? Just like that?"

Ebony finally turned. "It's not just like that."

Scotty's eyes were red-rimmed. "It is," he said. "One day, Dad dies, and now we're getting kicked out. That's what it feels like."

Ebony felt something flare up in her chest. Not anger. Not grief. Something like dignity. Something like a boundary.

"We are not getting kicked out," she said. "We are leaving because the alternative is worse."

"And what's worse?" Owen asked.

Ebony didn't answer. Because worse was sleeping with one eye open, wondering when the sheriff would show up. Worse was moving in with strangers who would love them just enough to judge them. Worse was hearing pity in every voice. Worse was Ebony waking up every morning and realizing she couldn't afford the life her husband died believing he left her.

"Leave it, Owen." Scotty inspected a bruised apple then tossed it into the trashcan. His calm trying to absorb Owen's heat.

"Don't tell me what to do," Owen snapped.

From the living room, Destiny began humming. Soft. Off-key. The same tune she'd been humming since the funeral, a hymn Ebony's mother used to sing while washing dishes.

Ebony exhaled slowly. "Destiny," she called, "Princess, you, okay?"

"I okay," Destiny answered brightly, like it was a question she'd been waiting to be asked.

Ebony rubbed her temple. "We're going to start packing today."

Owen stared at her like she'd betrayed him personally. "So, you're just gonna drag us to some backwards town because Dad's daddy—"

"Don't talk about him like that," Ebony snapped before she could stop herself.

Owen's mouth fell open a little.

Scotty's eyes widened.

Ebony rarely raised her voice. Even when she was angry, she tended to turn it inward and call it patience. She cleared her throat. "That man is your father's father," she said, slower now. "You can hate what he stands for. You can hate how he acts. But you will not speak his name like a curse in this house."

Owen's laugh was ugly. "In this house? Which house? The one we're losing?"

Ebony closed her eyes. She saw the letter again. She saw the bold print. She felt the paper slicing her future into pieces.

Then Destiny padded into the kitchen wearing ladybug slippers. She held something in her hands like it was sacred, a crumpled napkin with a crayon drawing on it. A stick figure family. Ebony knew the figures immediately because Destiny had given them color and ages. Ebony and Destiny were dark brown. The boys were a lighter brown. Her husband, Michael, had been crayoned yellow with a bright white smile and a stick hand holding Destiny's.

On the back of the paper she'd written, in careful, lopsided letters, the word—togefer. Destiny held it up. "Look, Mommy."

Ebony's throat tightened so hard she couldn't speak. She took the napkin gently, like it might crumble. "That's beautiful," she whispered.

Destiny beamed. "We stay *togefer*," she said again. Like a promise. Like a command.

Scotty turned away, rubbing his face hard with his sleeve. Owen looked down, jaw tight.

Ebony swallowed the ache and forced her voice steady. "We do."

Destiny climbed onto one of the kitchen chairs.

Ebony's eyes flicked to the space at the table where her husband used to sit. For a moment, it seemed as if he would walk in and take his place at the head of the table. She remembered the first time they ate at that table as a family of five. Destiny had been small, her cheeks full, her curls soft. She'd laughed so hard she snorted milk, and her husband. The way he'd laughed, had clapped his hands and said, "That's my girl." He'd always claimed Destiny with joy. He didn't treat her like fragile glass. He treated her like a gift. He treated all of them like a gift.

The memory caused Ebony's chest to hurt. She turned away from the chair before the tears returned. "Okay," she said briskly. "Everybody, go get trash bags. We're starting with the living room."

Scotty didn't move. "What about school?" he asked, quieter.

Ebony paused.

There it was, the real fear under the anger. Not football. Not friends. Not social media. The fear of being the new kid. The fear of being stared at. The fear of being half-seen and fully judged. "We'll finish this week," Ebony said. "Then we'll leave."

Scotty's eyes narrowed. "And what about… Dad's stuff?"

Ebony's hands went still.

Owen's gaze lifted to hers, and for the first time, she saw the question in his eyes, too. What do we do with the evidence of him? What do we do with the clothes that still smell like him? What do we do with a whole life that doesn't fit in boxes?

Ebony swallowed. "We pack what matters," she said softly. "We keep what we can."

"And what if we can't keep much?" Scotty asked quietly.

Ebony looked at her son, the boy who had become a young man in the span of a funeral. She felt both pride and grief and something like rage at the unfairness of it. "Then we keep each other," she said.

Scotty nodded once. Like he accepted that as a responsibility, not a comfort.

Destiny started humming again. Then she stopped and tilted her head, listening to something Ebony couldn't hear.

"What?" Ebony asked.

Destiny looked toward the living room. "Daddy chair," she said.

Ebony's stomach twisted. "What about Daddy's chair?"

Destiny pointed. "He not there," she said matter-of-factly, and then, as if that was not the end of the sentence, she added, "But God there."

Ebony's eyes stung.

Owen scoffed. "Destiny—"

Ebony cut him off with a look. She didn't have the energy to defend faith today, but she also didn't have the energy to let anyone stomp on Destiny's comfort.

Destiny hopped down and padded toward the living room, humming. Ebony followed. The living room was half-lit, dust dancing in the sunbeam. The couch was where it had always been. The throw blanket was still folded over the arm. The mantle still held the family photo and a jar of pennies her husband had been saving "for Destiny's first car," which had always made Ebony laugh and then, later, made her cry.

The empty chair sat in the corner by the bookshelf, his reading chair. Not missing. Just… empty. Ebony stared at it. She hadn't moved it since he died. She hadn't vacuumed under it. She hadn't even dusted the lamp beside it because touching it felt like admitting he wasn't coming back to sit there.

Destiny walked straight to it like it had called her by name. She stood in front of it and placed both palms on the armrest. "Bye," she said gently.

Ebony's breath caught.

Destiny turned and looked up at Ebony. "We go now," she said. "We go where God wants."

Ebony could've laughed at the simplicity of it, could've dismissed it as sweet theology coming from a child with Down syndrome. But something about the way Destiny stood there, steady and unafraid, made Ebony's spine straighten. Made her remember that leaving didn't mean losing everything. Sometimes leaving meant living. She stepped forward and touched the chair. Her fingers sank into the worn fabric, into the shape of him. She pictured his long legs stretched out, his socks mismatched, his book open on his knee. She pictured him looking up at her, smiling, as if the world didn't scare him.

She pictured him saying, "You can do hard things, Eb." A sound escaped her—half laugh, half sob.

Scotty appeared behind her. He didn't speak. He simply put a hand on her shoulder. Gentle, steady, the way her husband used to.

Owen stood in the doorway watching, arms crossed, trying to look bored. But his eyes were wet.

Ebony exhaled slowly. "All right," she said, voice rough. "We start here." She grabbed the trash bag Scotty had brought and held it open.

Destiny ran to the bookshelf and started pulling out children's books, stacking them in a neat pile. "These come," she declared.

Ebony wiped her eyes and smiled.

Owen went to the mantle and gently lifted the photo frame, as if it were fragile glass. He stared at it too long. Then he turned it face down, carefully, like he couldn't bear the eyes in the picture watching him pack.

Scotty moved at last, snatching up a box from the corner. He shoved random items inside—a candle, a remote, a pair of scissors. Angry packing. But packing.

Ebony watched them, their different griefs, their different ways of loving, and sensed the strangest thing bloom inside her. Not hope. Not yet. But motion. She went to the chair and, for the first time since the funeral, lifted the blanket draped over it. Underneath, on the seat cushion, was something she hadn't seen before. A folded piece of paper. Her breath caught. She reached for it with trembling fingers, unfolded it.

Her husband's handwriting. The words blurred as her eyes filled.

Scotty leaned closer. "Mom?"

Ebony couldn't speak. She pressed her palm over her mouth like she could hold herself together by force.

Scotty stepped up, eyes wide now. "What is it?"

Destiny tugged Ebony's sleeve. "Mommy?"

Ebony lowered the paper and forced herself to read aloud the note that looked as if it had been hastily written.

Dear Ebony,

I'm sorry. I tried to fix things.

I tried to leave you a way through.

It's in the barn.

As you know, the will is with our lawyer,

and so is my life insurance policy.

So please settle things with him.

You and the kids will be okay.

I promise.

The house in Home, North Carolina,

was left to you. But whatever you do,

don't trust my father or Gabe.

Love,

Michael

Scotty's hand tightened on her shoulder. "The barn?" he repeated.

Ebony stared at the words until they felt carved into her skin. Outside, the Colorado wind pressed against the windows like it wanted in. Ebony folded the note with careful hands. She looked at her children. Owen, suddenly alert. Scotty, suddenly afraid. Destiny, blinking up at her with pure, steady trust. Ebony's heart raced. It wasn't just foreclosure. It wasn't just grief. Something else had been moving in the dark. What was Michael talking about? He'd never mentioned a life insurance policy before, and when she'd met with the lawyer. The savings and house that'd been left to her had been drained to cover Michael's medical expenses after his company let him go in the middle of chemo treatment. Sure, he'd left her the childhood home that his father had given to him, but it had been several years since she'd been back. The old house and barn could've been in shambles for all she knew.

Scotty shook his head. "I thought the lawyer said there was nothing left."

"Okay," she said, voice low and firm as a vow. "We pack."

Owen's eyes narrowed. "Mom, what did Dad mean?"

Ebony looked toward the door, toward the horizon, toward the road that waited.

"I don't know," she whispered. "But we're going to find out."

Destiny smiled like she'd been waiting for Ebony to say it. "We go," Destiny said.

Ebony nodded. "Yes," she said. "We go."

For the first time since her husband's death, Ebony didn't feel as if she were only running.

She felt as if she might be walking into a truth that had been waiting for her all along.

Chapter 3

Destiny

I don lik boxez. Boxez mean things are goin away.

In Colarado, we only had boxez at Chrismas, and that was ok becuz boxez   mint prezants and Daddy ~~pretindng~~ pretandng he didnt no what was insidevn tho he alwys did. Daddy was bad at pretandng. He wood smil too sun.

Now ther are boxez evrywher. Brown ones. Big ones. Sum say KITCHEN in thck black markr. Sum say BOOKS. One says DESTINY in Mom's hanwritng. I traced my nam with my fingr and the markr felt bumpe and dry.

Daddy's not her to help tape them shut. Daddy dieed a munth ago. I don't like saying that word. Dieed felz sharpe in my muth. Like bitng a chip the wron way. Peple say "pased away," but that sonds like he jus walked pas us in the halway and fourgot to say hi. Daddy woodnt do that. He alwys said hi. Evnif he was tired. Evn if he was lat.

I still think he might cum thru the dor sumtimes. Expecaly when it's qiate.

It's not qiate much anemur.

Mom movez fast now. Fast like she's in a rase she didnt sign up four. Her hair stays in a messe bun and she fourgets to drink her cofee. I no becuz I see the cups half full on the conter. Daddy uzed to tese her about that. He said cofee was ~~expansave~~ expinsive to wast.

Owen is 18 and triez to act like hes not sad. He got taler this year. Taler than Daddy. He stans in dorways like he's garding us. He talks to Mom in low voicez at niht when he thinks Scotty and I can hair. I can hair. My ears wurkvere well.

Scotty is 16 and mad at everythin. He punches his pilow. He runs outsid and cumz back swety and doesnt say why. He doesnt like when peple at church say, "Your the man of the hose now." I don think he wants that job.

I don want to muv. But maybee it wil be fun. Mom says were muvin to Norf Caralina. To a town called HOME. That is so funne. We are leavin home to go to HOME.

I axed her that and she smild but her eyes got shiney. "It wll be gud for us, Princes," she said. She stil calls me that. Daddy did two. Scotty says it's ~~emberasang~~ embarasang but I don car.

I paked Lady B myslf. Lady B is my stufed ladybug. She has one buton eye and one ~~stitked~~ stchitched eye becuz Butons feell off when I was 9 and Daddy fixxed her. He said she luked toufer that way. Like shed seen things.

Ladybugs are my favarote becuz they are smal but brihgt. Red with blckdots. They don look like there supozed to surviv wintr, but they do. Daddy tol me ladybugs are gud luck. I axed him if we still had gud lck. He said yes. That was befor.

The last niht in Calarado, I lay on my bed witout shets becuz they were alredy pcked. The matres felt ~~seretchy~~ stracty. I culd see the sqar on the wall wher my butterfly postr uzed to hang. The air smeled like cardbord and dust. So I got up and axed O and Bobo and mom to sleep in the livng rum and they siad yes!!

I whispeered to Lady B, "Were goin to HOME." I trid to imagan it. I imagan a big sign that says WELCOME HOME and evryone claps when you arriv. I imaganed sunflowerz becuz I saw a picturonce in a magizine at the doctrs ofic. I imaganed peple who talk slow and swet like honey.

I also imaganed kids who star at me. Sutimes kids star. They luk at my eyez two long or the way I move my hands when I'm excitd. In Calarado, my techer, Ms. Boyd, wood say, "Destiny, luk at me," and I wood and she wood smil lik evrythin was ezactly how it shuld be. I don no who my new techer is. I don no if she will lik ladybugs.

Chapter 4

Owen slammed his shoulder into his younger brother as he folded his six-foot-three frame into the second row of the SUV. Two grieving siblings pressed together, neither willing to give ground.

"Why do I have to sit in the back with *him*?" My oldest son asked, his green eyes flashing against copper-colored skin.

I rubbed my aching temples and unclenched my teeth. "Because I said so."

Scotty tugged his soccer cap low, the brim hiding his eyes but not the sniffles he failed to control. He looked like a younger, three-inch-shorter version of his brother Owen. Same build, same sharp cheekbones—but with the fair complexion of his Irish father and my dark brown eyes. Though he was still growing, years of soccer had carved muscle into his legs and shoulders.

Both boys were tall. Both lean. Both hurting.

I readjusted my mirrors and observed Owen lean close and whisper something to his brother.

"That's not nice to call people *baby* when they're not," Destiny said. "Right, mommy?"

"That's right, honey."

Scotty turned away from Owen. "Just leave me alone."

I finished angling my rearview and spun around. "Stop, Owen. We've got a long drive ahead of us, and I don't need you or anyone else making it any harder than it has to be."

I exhaled as my threat was met with icy silence. The early morning slipped behind us as we passed the "Sold" sign staked into the front yard. Colorado faded in the rearview mirror as we headed East—toward North Carolina, toward a life none of us had chosen.

The SUV carried my three children and what little remained of our lives. No room for thirteen-year-old Destiny's swing set. No room for sixteen-year-old Scotty's dirt bike. And certainly, no room for the half-rebuilt '66 Mustang engine my nineteen-year-old had poured years into rebuilding with his father.

I sensed that we all felt the absence of Michael. My husband of nineteen years, buried last November at Memorial Gardens.

I glanced in the rearview mirror. Owen's scowl stared back at me.

"You're in the back because all of you insisted that we bring the TV instead of shipping it with the moving truck," I said. "The front seat is the safest place for the flat screen."

"Should've sold it and shipped the engine instead," Owen muttered.

"No one cares about your stupid motor," Scotty said.

I slammed on the brakes.

Seatbelts snapped tight, bodies lurched forward, and beside me the fifty-five-inch HD plasma—wrapped in quilts like a fragile infant—didn't move an inch.

I twisted in my seat. "Enough!" I said, my voice low and sharp. "I have no problem letting the neighbors watch me rearrange this truck again just to put *you*"—my eyes locked on Owen— "in the very back with the luggage."

"A lot of good that'll do when you need me to drive."

"I never said I needed your help."

He's right, though. Fifteen hours to Missouri is more than I can manage alone. Michael would've had us on the road by four. Calm. Efficient. Smiling.

Our first trip without my spouse was turning into anything but peaceful. "Okay," I said quietly. "Truce, Owen." I couldn't afford to push him further. His father had always known how to reach him. And his father was gone.

Destiny whimpered softly, pressing her stuffed ladybug—Lady B—against her face. The only one of my children with my dark complexion. She'd refused to let me braid her hair that morning and wore two wavy ponytails halfway down her back. Change rattled her. It rattled me, too.

Scotty lifted his cap and met my eyes, red-rimmed and apologetic. "Sorry, Mom."

Always the first to apologize. Even when he wasn't at fault.

Owen huffed, turned toward the window, shoved earbuds in, and slid down in his seat. Communication over.

Destiny reached for Scotty's arm. "Don't cry, Bobo."

"I'm okay, Desi." He gently pulled away.

She smiled anyway and turned back to the window. Brokenness didn't linger long in her world.

The neighborhood disappeared behind us, replaced by thoughts of Michael. Wasn't *till death do us part* supposed to mean old age?

Empty nests. Grandchildren. Weren't we supposed to grow old together?

Michael Scott McMullen had proposed six months before my twenty-first birthday. We married six months later.

"Best birthday gift ever," he'd said on our wedding night. "And the girl of my dreams all rolled into one."

Gold flecks danced in his green eyes—the same eyes he passed to our oldest son.

"Let's grow old together, Mr. McMullen," I'd whispered.

"I promise, Mrs. McMullen."

So much for promises.

Old age wasn't supposed to look like a forty-three-year-old African American widow gripping the steering wheel of an overpacked SUV. I wiped my cheeks, turned on the radio, and prayed the signal would last past the city limits. Prayed God would prepare me for small-town North Carolina and for a father-in-law who'd never forgiven me for existing.

When the kids finally fell asleep, relief washed over me. I turned the volume down and breathed. No fighting. No tears. No guilt—at least for a little while.

I glanced back at Owen. Stubble shadowed his jaw beneath high cheekbones. Loose curls like his father's fell to his shoulders. Even asleep, his face carried anger and grief. Black T-shirt. Jeans. Armor.

Scotty slept on, his soft snores steady and small, while Owen leaned into him, his head hiding the worn soccer emblem like one more piece of their old life neither of them quite knew how to hold anymore.

As obedient as one son was defiant, the other bent inward. I fought the urge to compare them.

Destiny sucked softly, a habit she never outgrew. At four-foot-nine, she looked younger than thirteen. The doctors said she likely wouldn't grow much taller.

Michael had wanted a third child.

"A little princess," he'd said, hands resting on my belly. "Just like her mother."

"Or a third prince."

He laughed. "No. This one's a girl."

"Do you have a name, know-it-all?"

"Destiny."

"Why?"

"There's something special about her."

She arrived during a February storm. Michael raced through a blizzard to get us to the hospital. Moments after her birth, the room fell quiet.

"Michael?" I called.

His back was to me as nurses rushed past. Our baby's cries were small, weak against the noise of the room.

Despite the pain, I pushed myself upright. "Michael… what's wrong?"

He turned, fear filling his eyes. "Our daughter was diagnosed with Down syndrome."

The memory still lingers in quiet moments—like now.

"Mama."

Destiny's reflection caught mine in the rearview mirror as she signed *food*, her hands sure and familiar. She rarely signed with anyone but me anymore. I reached into the cooler beside me for a granola bar and held it up.

She shook her head.

I traded the granola bar for a small bag of yogurt-covered raisins.

She giggled.

"Thank you," Destiny said when I slipped the snack to her.

"You're welcome, Princess."

I checked my watch. It'd been less than two hours into our drive. I hoped the raisins would buy us time.

"I'll take the granola bar," Scotty said, leaning forward.

I saw his fingers wiggling behind me in my peripheral vision. "Wait, are you buckled in, son?"

"Yeah, just not the shoulder belt." He yawned. "It's too tight."

I fished the granola bar from the cooler and tossed it behind me.

Scotty finished his food in two bites and reached for another snack.

"Should I be looking for a place to eat?" I asked Scotty as I passed the bar to give Destiny to her brother.

I glanced into my rearview and watched as he shrugged and chewed.

Static crept into the radio—distance announcing itself. I turned it off.

"Son, you do realize that I can't read your mind and—"

"Why'd you make him come?"

"I didn't force Owen. You of all people know he couldn't stay in Greenwood."

The judge's words echoed. *Maybe it's best to relocate your family, Mrs. McMullen.*

"He hates you for leaving our Dad there."

There. The cemetery.

I tightened my grip on the wheel.

"What about you, do you hate me?"

Scotty was quiet for several seconds as thunder rolled in the distance. "No, I don't, Mom," he said.

My shoulders eased.

"But I don't understand."

Neither do I.

To distract myself from the emotions overwhelming me, I ripped open a bag of pretzels and stuffed a handful into my dry mouth. A single tear still managed to escape as we drove past a vast open field. Wind kicked dirt into a small spiral before it settled again. The sky darkened as the first rumble of thunder followed us East.

Chapter 5

Two hours later, we stopped. Rain sheeted past the windshield wipers at the rundown chain restaurant. It wasn't my favorite food establishment, but it was a step up from other fast-food places, and it would give us a chance to get out of the car.

Thunder rumbled across the sky like a low growl in the throat of an angry beast.

With each lightning flash, Destiny struck a pose. "Cheese," she said, as if someone were taking her picture.

I smiled, suddenly thankful for a daughter who'd never been afraid of storms, even though plenty of other fears filled her life. Rolling my stiff shoulders back, I glanced around for the umbrella I kept in the car.

"Any idea where the umbrella is?" I asked, feeling beneath my seat, but turned up with nothing.

"Won't do any good in this monsoon," Owen said.

I stared behind me at my oldest, who still appeared to be asleep.

He opened his eyes enough to show he was ready to pick up where we'd left off. "Staring at me won't do any good either."

Too weary to fight, I turned to Scotty. "Son, would you check the back?"

He turned and glanced at the wall of boxes and luggage in the rear of the vehicle. "Where?"

Fingers intertwined behind my neck, pulled against the tension. "Never mind. Okay, on a count of three, let's run for the door."

"Just go." Owen opened his door and stepped into the downpour. "Or not."

Scotty handed me his baseball cap. "Here, Mom."

"Thanks." Tears blurred my vision at his effort to help. Michael would have done the same thing.

He scooted across the seat and hurried after his brother.

Cap on, purse in hand, I turned to face Destiny. "It's you and me, kid."

Lightning flashed.

Destiny smiled. "Cheese."

By the time we entered, the guys were already being led to a table. The cap did little good. The only thing dry was the contents of my purse. Voices mingled in the air, creating a morning hum. We walked past a table with plates of French toast and breakfast skillets, onions, sausages, cheese, and other ingredients. At a quick glance, it was the perfect combination of delicious scents. *Maybe this dive wasn't such a bad choice after all.* Waitresses at different tables filled cups with coffee, allowing me to inhale their rich, bold aroma.

"Yum." Destiny gazed around the restaurant.

The waitress waited until we were seated, Destiny next to me and the guys across, then handed us menus.

She shifted in my direction and held her pen over an order pad.

"I'll take your drink orders first. Can I get you some coffee, ma'am?"

"Yeah," Owen replied.

How could one word carry so much disrespect? I stared at Owen as he kept his eyes focused on the menu. "Two, please."

She turned to Scotty.

"Mom, can I get hot chocolate?"

"Sure," I said, trying not to tally our waning funds.

Black nails gripped her pen. The name badge on her uniform read Tami. She wrote down Scotty's order and addressed me as she studied Destiny. "What will your daughter have, ma'am?"

I rubbed my burning eyes and tried focusing on the menu instead of Tami. "My daughter is capable of telling you what she wants."

Destiny folded her hands on the table and sat up straight. "I'll have white chocolate."

Tami arched a brow. "Excuse me?"

I met the waitress's heavily lined eyes. "It's simple, Tami. White chocolate is milk warmed like cocoa, with a dash of vanilla flavoring. I'll add the sugar."

Her cheeks flushed. "Back in a moment with, um, your drinks." Tami shoved the pen behind her ear and turned away to reveal large black star tattoos across her neck, something her spiked hair couldn't hide. Complete with a nape piercing.

"So, who's the real freak?" Owen stared after her. He angled his seat, hooked his arm on the back of his chair as he tilted back. "I'm sure it'll only get better the closer we get to North Carolina."

"Five minutes." I planted my trembling hands on the table and leaned over. "That's all I ask. Can you please stuff your attitude for five minutes? You know how it is. We go through this all the time."

Owen let his chair drop with a thud.

"No one should treat Destiny that way. Ignore her like she doesn't exist." He propped his forearms on the table. "Dad would've put Tami in her place."

His words stabbed. He resumed his previous position and looked away.

Destiny patted my arm numerous times to the point of stinging. Hard to give her attention after another confrontation with Owen.

She pointed to a picture on the menu. "Pancakes?"

"Yes."

Her expression was full of excitement. "With blueberries?"

"Of course," I said and stood as our waitress approached. "I'm running to the bathroom. I'll be back."

"Mom, what do you want to eat?" Scotty asked.

"I don't care. Order for me," I said over my shoulder. "Just don't forget Destiny wants pancakes with blueberries."

I followed the bathroom signs like they were a way, clipping a waitress so closely, she gasped and tilted her tray. I didn't stop. Once I entered the empty lady's room, I locked the door of the roomy handicapped stall and slid down the wall, months of grief breaking loose in hot tears.

Surrendering to the quiet collapse, more tears came unchecked, a release I'd denied for months. The bathroom became my temporary refuge. An altar built of cracked tile and despair.

Leaving Colorado felt like exile. Whatever God had once promised us there lay unfinished, half-buried beneath disappointment. And now I was leading my family forward, not with certainty, but with fear, toward a place that didn't feel chosen, only endured. I sat there for what seemed like hours, but after checking my watch, it'd only been fifteen minutes. Still, if I didn't return to my family, they'd soon come looking for me.

"Lord, did I mishear you?" I silently asked as I washed and dried my face, but no answer came, at least not in the way I could understand.

Back at the table, the restaurant's noise rose like static, filling the hollow where prayer had failed. Destiny finished her pancakes and reached for my eggs, unaware of the quiet unravelling across from her. I managed half a slice of toast and a few bites of bacon before my body refused any more. Scotty finished the rest. I drank a fourth cup of coffee, asking it to do what faith could not in that moment—keep me standing.

By the time we prepared to leave, the rain had stopped, and the sun beat down on the pavement. The air was thick with the smell of wet asphalt, rising in steam from the parking lot.

After settling Destiny into her seat with the ladybug pillow and books to read, I closed her door and almost bumped into Owen who stood by the opened driver's door.

"Owen—"

"Let me drive, Mom. You're tired." He held his hand out for the keys, furrowed his brow, this time not in anger, but concern.

I handed him the keys. "Fine," I said, resisting the urge to reach up and stroke his cheek the way I'd done when he was younger. Instead, I walked to the rear passenger's side, where Scotty held the door open for me.

His expression was somewhere between that of a boy and that of a man. *When did his eyes grow to be so sad?* "Thanks, honey." I squeezed his arm. Then crawled into the middle seat.

Destiny patted her shoulder. "Sleep here, Mama," she whispered, her breath smelling of maple syrup. When I rested my head on her shoulder, I inhaled the lavender scent of her favorite bath gel that lingered on her skin.

She opened a worn picture book. "I'll read to you."

But before Destiny finished the second page, she fell asleep. I gently took the children's book from her and tucked it into the backseat pocket. Watching her mouth form a smile, I closed my eyes and remembered years earlier when Michael walked through the back door and scooped a then six-year-old Destiny off the kitchen barstool and into his arms.

She giggled and squirmed against his tickle attack.

He rubbed his nose against hers. "Whatcha doing, Princess?"

With fingers spread, she held up her tiny fingers covered in flour. "Cooking with Mama." Destiny placed her hands on the sides of her father's beard and rubbed her nose against his.

My smile came easily then as I prepared chicken cutlets for dinner.

Michael set Destiny back on her stool, and she returned to tracing slow circles in the flour dusting the counter, white against the worn surface. He took a glass from the cabinet and came to the sink beside me. The faucet ran. He filled the glass and drank deeply, as if something inside him had gone dry. He filled it again, drank halfway, then stopped, breath caught, shoulders lowering.

"Are you okay?" I asked.

"Yeah, it's like I'm dying of thirst." He leaned toward me, close, offering himself without a word. I brushed the flour from his beard, a small act of undoing. He frowned and lifted his arm to his forehead, wiping at the day, at the weight, as though water alone might cleanse what neither of us could name.

"Do you still have a fever?"

"It's nothing. I think I just caught some kind of bug." He finished his water.

"I really wish you'd go see Dr. Calhoun."

"Ebony, I've told you before," he cleared his throat. "The McMullen men never get sick."

He stood tall, accentuating the nine-inch difference between us.

"Really?" I frowned and slowly eased a packet of fettuccini noodles into the boiling pot. "More like, you McMullen men *never* seem to listen to reason."

Just then, Owen ran into the kitchen with a basketball.

"Hey, Dad," he said, his voice cracking. At twelve, he was entering puberty and hopefully growing into his size fourteen feet. "Want to shoot some hoops with me?"

"Why?" Michael arched a thick brow. "Do you want to take down your old man again?"

Owen grinned. "Something like that. Mom, did he tell you? I beat him yesterday."

Michael flushed and wiped sweat near his hairline. "Yeah, our boy beat up on me when I'm not at my best. What kind of victory is that?"

Owen tossed the ball to his dad. "A sweet one."

Michael caught the pass, threw his head back, and laughed. One of the things I loved most about my husband was his deep, embracing laughter. "Not today, buddy," he said and shook his head before tossing the ball back to our son. "I think your old man needs a nap."

Owen's shoulders drooped. "Maybe later?"

"We'll see," Michael said, ignoring the scowl I leveled at him. He brushed my cheek with a quick kiss before slipping out of the kitchen.

I packed the last piece of seasoned chicken—extra garlic, of course, a non-negotiable in the McMullen house—into a Tupperware container. My hands shaking slightly. I walked to the sink to wash off the flour, wondering how to convince the man I loved to see a doctor, even though he refused to see the danger.

A sudden crash from the other room made me jump, my heart leaping into my throat.

"Owen Michael McMullen! If you bounced that ball and broke something. So, help me, I will make you wish—"

"Mom, come quick! Something's wrong with Dad!"

I nearly knocked the chicken from the counter as I tore down the hall, my heart hammering in my chest.

Destiny followed, her tiny footsteps an echo of mine.

Our bedroom looked like the aftermath of a storm. Michael lay motionless on the hardwood, Owen crouched beside him, hands trembling under his father's head as if holding him together could keep him alive. Papers and pens littered the floor like confetti from some cruel celebration. A lamp had toppled, its base cracked, and glass splintered across the rug. Our recent family portrait lay in ruin, the shattered frame slicing through the image of us, leaving only fragments staring back.

I froze, every nerve screaming. Time slowed, the world narrowed to the sight of my husband, broken and still, and the boy who loved him enough to try to hold him together.

Destiny pleaded, "Daddy, please wake up."

I crouched down next to them and touched my husband's pale cheek. His fever had spiked higher. "Michael? Wake up, honey. You're scaring us," I said as I rubbed his chest, wishing he were playing one of his jokes on us. But he remained unresponsive.

Choking back tears, I gestured to my son. "Quick, get my phone!"

Owen froze, his red eyes focused on his father.

"Owen!"

As if in a trance, Owen removed his hand from beneath his father's head.

I tried without success to stifle my scream when I saw that Owen's palms were covered in blood.

My body jerked from the remnants of the nightmare, heart thudding in the quiet hum of the car. To my left, Destiny hugged her pillow, small and silent against the seat. On my right, Scotty's leg pressed against mine, his head resting against the window, warm breath fogging the glass as Owen sped down the freeway.

"As much coffee as you drank, I'm surprised you slept." Owen's eyes met mine in the rearview. "Sounds like you were having a bad dream, though."

"I was."

"What was it about?" He pulled an earbud from his ear. "Was it about the injustice of what you're doing to our family?"

I reached for my water bottle and took a swig, choosing to ignore the bait. "Where are we?"

"The flatlands."

I checked the road signs but couldn't see anything that told me where we were. "Can you be more specific?"

"The *ugly* flatlands."

I shook my head and let my gaze drift out the window. Oil drills bobbed in the distance, their long steel arms dipping and rising like endless drinking birds, forever chasing a liquid they could never reach. Beyond them, a field of corn stretched to the horizon, a sea of gold and green that rippled in the wind. Another swath of land held a low, plush crop, its form so uniform it blurred into a soft, indistinct carpet.

"We're about thirty minutes until Salina," Owen said.

"Thanks, son." I checked my watch and did a rough calculation. "We still have over eight hours before we reach Gabe's." He's the kids' favorite, and only, uncle.

Owen smirked as he whizzed past two enormous rigs. "Not if I'm driving."

"I don't expect you to drive the entire way. In fact, I'm ready to take it from here," I mumbled as we sped by several more cars. *Please, Lord, no unmarked police vehicles.*

"I may as well drive." He tapped the steering wheel with his fingers. "It's not like I've got anything else to do," Owen said and shoved his earbud back into place.

I fought against the tug of my seatbelt to reach over and tap his shoulder.

He removed one of the earbuds, an irritated expression on his face. "What?"

"Take them out."

"Why?"

"It's illegal."

"That was Colorado, we're in Kansas."

"It doesn't matter what state we're in. As long as you're driving *my* car, take them out."

Owen glanced over his shoulder, yanked his other earbud out, held them up in the rearview mirror for display, then dropped them on the seat.

"Thank you. Now was that so hard?"

"Whatever," he muttered, switching on the radio and scanning until he landed on a station he liked. Then he cranked the volume up to fill the front of the SUV.

I dug my nails into my knees to keep from snapping, bouncing my leg until Scotty reached over and rested his hand on my knee.

His eyes were still closed, but a grin tugged at his lips. He fished a pack of gum from his pocket and offered one.

I popped the gum into my mouth, balled up the wrapper, and flicked it at the back of Owen's head—but his curls caught it like a tiny shield.

Scotty chuckled and sat up. He glanced around before whispering. "Where are we?"

"About eight hours 'til Uncle Gabe's."

"Any more stops before we get there?"

Destiny yawned, shifted in her seat and squeezed her pillow.

"How about a late lunch with ice cream for dinner?" I whispered, hoping to allow Destiny to sleep for as long as possible.

Scotty twisted his wrists outward, causing them to pop like small firecrackers. "Works for me." He reached between the door and his leg and pulled out a large bag of chips, an almost empty one.

"Where'd you get those?"

He popped a handful of chips into his mouth. "Owen treated Destiny and me when we stopped for gas."

"I slept through that?"

"Yep," he said and offered me some of his chips. "Owen filled the tank. He said he wasn't stopping until we were out of Kansas."

I grabbed a handful of chips. "He paid for gas?" I asked, my voice lowered. "With what?"

"Your credit card." Scotty patted my knee. "But don't worry. He didn't buy anything else. And he used his money to buy my chips and Destiny's cookies."

Nodding, I reached into the bag and took out more chips than intended. "I'll buy you more."

"I've eaten most of them." He handed over the bag.

"You sure?"

"I ate your breakfast."

"Right."

Scotty reached into the backpack between his feet and drew out an electric device, a gift from his dad. My middle child had always been a reader, the one who lingered in the quiet corners of the world, finding light in stories when the rest of life felt too loud. Nights spent beneath his covers, one more chapter always calling him forward, were his small acts of devotion—to imagination, to himself. Flashlights and extra chargers rested in a box under his bed, tokens of preparedness, of hope tucked away in secret. Perhaps he had glimpsed my stash while searching for one of Destiny's toys. Occasionally, I would add a new charger, silent offerings, and he never asked. That unspoken trust, that quiet acknowledgment of care and foresight, felt almost sacred, like a prayer passing without sound between parent and child.

Michael shared many of the same adventure and fantasy books as our second-born. On Sunday afternoons after church, they would disappear into the study, voices rising and falling with the excitement of imagined worlds. Michael had a way of drawing out our quiet child through laughter, gentle banter, debates over a character's choices or the weapons they wielded, even the fantastical question of how a lightsaber might fare in battle. If those walls could speak, they would whisper of a father's love, patient and steady, and of the small, perfect magic that unfolded whenever imagination and connection met.

But even in that moment, the memory of the hardwood floor in our bedroom lingered in my chest. Michael lying still, Destiny's soft whimpering, Owen cradling his head, the shattered lamp and glass glinting like warning signs. That laughter, that warmth, felt fragile now, hanging by the thinnest thread. And I knew, as I watched them together, that the world could tilt in an instant—and there was nothing I could do to hold it steady.

Chapter 6

Late in the afternoon, we agreed to lunch at a popular fast-food restaurant, where Destiny would be able to play after eating.

My daughter hurried through her meal. With a nugget stuffed in her cheek, she handed me her last one and darted for the play area.

"Fifteen minutes," I called after her.

She nodded without turning around. Her two pigtails, now curlier from the rain, bounced against her back.

As I finished my salad, my focus shifted to my sons, who were inhaling their second burger. "I'm going outside to see if I can touch base with Gabe and give him an update."

Scotty crammed a handful of fries into his mouth. "Are you still planning on stopping at a hotel tonight?"

"I'm pretty sure we'll need to stop for the night, but let's see how Destiny does when the sun starts to set." I picked up my trash, slung my pocketbook over my shoulder, and stood. "When you two finish up, can you please grab your sister? I'll be by the car."

"Sure, Mom," Scotty answered.

Owen scowled. "When we tell her it's time to leave, I'm sure she's going to be thrilled. Then what?"

"If she puts up a fuss, let her know I've got a pack of new stickers for her in the car," I said before leaving.

Once I got to the car, I realized Owen still had the keys. I leaned against the driver's door for a few seconds before the heat of the metal assaulted my back. Moving to the back of the SUV in search of shade, I sat on the bumper and called my brother-in-law.

"Gabriel's Movers. Gabe here."

"Got a sec?"

"Sure, Eb. Just hang on for a few. I'll be right back." Country music played in the background of Gabe's office phone. I shifted the cell to my other hand and massaged my temple with the free one.

"Sorry about that," Gabe's cheerful voice boomed. "Got a stranded truck. That was the driver giving me an update."

"It wasn't the one with our stuff, I hope."

"No, this one's headed to Arizona."

I exhaled. "Thank you. I couldn't do any of this without you."

"No problem. Did everything fit?"

"Minus a swing set, dirt bike, and car engine."

Gabe whistled. "So, Owen sold the engine?"

"Not willingly, but what choice did I have?"

He laughed. "I get it, but I'm sure that didn't make you very popular with him," Gabe said and coughed. A nervous tic he displayed when worried. "So, are you guys ready for bachelor cooking tonight?"

"That's why I'm calling. We're in Kansas, stopped at a fast-food place outside Salina," I checked her watch and sighed. "That means we still have several hours left—"

"Which would get y'all here around midnight with minimal stops. That's pretty late, Eb. Ain't it?"

I stared at the ground, watching an ant struggle with dragging a piece of a French fry. "We'll probably need to stop."

"No problem." Gabe coughed. "My stew is always better the next day anyway."

"What about the moving truck?" I asked and wiped a bead of sweat from my forehead. "If we stop, we'll be an entire day later than planned."

"Don't worry. I've already got it covered."

"How so?"

"Owen reached out to me earlier today when you were sleeping. I've already contacted your driver."

I turned to stare at my sons. Owen was coercing Destiny to leave the ball pit with Scotty behind him. "Wow, thank you. I'll keep you posted."

"I know a lot has happened, Eb." Gabe coughed. "But you got some great kids. It'll work out. You'll see," he said before ending the call.

I shoved the phone into my purse and waited. The ant I'd been watching earlier struggled across the pavement, dragging a fry toward a crack. It forced the food through, disappeared, then emerged on the other side and kept going.

The fissure in the concrete mirrored the one opening inside me. I didn't know if there was a way through—or only a fall.

Once we got into the car and back onto the highway, Destiny whimpered as the sky bled from blue to gray. In the rearview mirror, she clutched her pillow, eyes wide, searching the dark for something I couldn't see. The clouds closed in as the last light slipped away.

"Desi, would you like to listen to music?" I fumbled through my purse for her headphones, eyes locked on the dark ribbon of highway ahead.

In the rearview mirror, Destiny squeezed her eyes shut and shook her head. "I want to go home."

"Princess, we're only minutes from a hotel." Minutes could feel like forever to a child afraid of the dark. The last color drained from the sky. No stars yet—only clouds closing in.

She lowered her pillow just enough for me to see her trembling mouth. "It's dark, Mama."

"I know. I'm trying." I pressed the accelerator, passing a sign—Columbia, four exits. "Hey," I said too brightly, "you can play a game on my phone."

Scotty leaned toward her. We both knew what would happen if this spiraled.

"I'm scared, Bobo."

"I'm here, Desi." His arm wrapped around her.

I mouthed, "Thank you," and clicked the radio on. I searched for classical—Vivaldi, Bach, anything familiar—but the stations dissolved into static.

"Mom." Scotty's voice was low.

In the mirror, Destiny was shaking.

I tossed my purse into the back. "Scotty, please find her headphones," I said, softening my voice. "Princess, want to listen to music?"

When Scotty shifted his arm, Destiny's fear exploded. Her whimper rose into a scream.

"No! Too dark! Home, Mama—now!" She clawed at the seatbelt. Reached for the door.

"Scotty, stop her!" I cut across three lanes, horns blaring, searching for an exit. The sky swallowed the last of the light as Scotty fought to hold her.

"Ouch—Destiny, stop!"

I glanced back, observing red welts blooming on Scotty's cheek. I took the exit too fast, ignored the stop sign, and jerked onto the gravel of a Mini-Mart. I left my door open and yanked Destiny's door wide.

She kicked—hard. The blow knocked the air from my lungs and dropped me to my knees. Another foot flew past my face. Her eyes were squeezed shut, her body wild with terror. "Destiny." I gasped. "Look at me."

She couldn't hear me.

Scotty held her from behind, one arm tight around her waist, the other pressed to his bleeding cheek. Owen stepped out of the SUV and came to stand behind me.

"Destiny Marie," he said. Calm. Steady. Commanding. "Look at the stars."

Her body stilled. "Stars?" she whispered.

Owen patted her shoulder. "Yes, Desi."

I prayed he wasn't guessing.

She opened her eyes a sliver. "Where?" Her gaze followed something behind me.

"Only two?" Her shoulders dropped.

"More to come." Owen hadn't sounded that gentle in years.

I pressed my forehead to Destiny's knees, fighting for breath, for control. She turned away and signed that she needed to use the bathroom.

"I know," I said, and helped her out of the car. She walked with me to the trunk. I opened it and reached for the emergency bag I hadn't needed since Michael's funeral, praying it held clean clothes.

Before we walked inside, I looked back.

Scotty wiped blood from his cheek.

Owen leaned against the open door, the streetlight flickering on and off above him. "Go," he said quietly. "I've got this."

I took Destiny's hand and headed toward the Mini-Mart—not knowing what this was, or what would be waiting when I came back.

Chapter 7

In the cramped bathroom, I rinsed the last traces of filth and fear from Destiny's skin, warm water circling the drain. Her soiled clothes lay knotted in a plastic bag atop the open trash, along with my silent promise to replace her butterfly-print pants. The once rancid air now smelled of soap and relief. She glanced once at the bag, then bowed her head. "I'm sorry, Mama."

Outside the bathroom, I lifted her chin until our eyes met—those almond-shaped eyes people judged too quickly, framed by lashes so long they brushed her brow. I cupped her cheek, my thumb passing over the dimple that appeared when she smiled. "Sorry for what?"

She looked away. "For being a scaredy-cat."

"Sometimes being scared is the only thing we can be," I said gently. "And sometimes it gets messy. I'm always here. Okay?"

She nodded against my shirt.

At the Mini-Mart doors, she stopped. The night pressed in beyond the glass. She squeezed my hand.

"Do you want Mama to carry you?" *Could I?* Michael could have—easily.

She stepped back as the doors slid shut.

I tugged her hand. "Destiny, we can't stay here."

A man brushed past us, energy drink in hand, irritation on his face. "You're blocking the way."

I glared at him and swallowed. "I have an idea."

Minutes later, we headed back to the SUV armed with three flashlights and far too many batteries. One light strapped to Destiny's head like a miner's lamp, two clutched in her hands. Even so, she pressed into my side, eyes squeezed shut, nearly taking us both down.

Scotty leaned against the SUV, arms crossed, smiling.

"What?" I asked.

"You found those in there?"

"Clearance," Destiny said, adjusting her headlamp.

When I tried to guide her into the car, she braced herself against the open door.

"Please no, Mama. It's too dark."

"Princess, we need to find a hotel."

"No." She dug in, breath shaking.

"I don't know what to do," I whispered.

"Mom." Scotty pointed past the Mini-Mart. "Owen went to check."

Across the lot, a motel sign glowed.

A laugh and a sob escaped me at once.

Owen emerged from the darkness moments later. "They've got a room." Relief barely settled before he turned back toward the shadows.

"Can one of you carry her?" I asked.

Scotty lifted Destiny. She wrapped her arms around his neck, holding tight as the light flickered. "Don't choke me, Desi," he said and pulled to loosen his sister's grip as he walked toward the motel. Destiny's legs were locked around Scotty's waist as he carried her past the gas pumps toward our motel for the night.

Owen trailed behind them.

I drew a deep breath and started the car, fighting the exhaustion settling into my bones. "How much more, God?" I asked, wishing I could get an answer. An audible one. The drive from the Mini-Mart took seconds.

Owen waited as I maneuvered into a parking spot by the hotel's entrance.

"If we'd stopped an hour ago, this wouldn't have happened," he said as soon as I opened my door.

"Thanks for the advice." I slammed the door shut. "Where are the other two?"

"The lobby." Owen pointed at the motel and grabbed his camo bag.

I dragged out the blue duffel, Destiny, and I shared, then lifted Scotty's black bag. It dropped hard at my feet. *What on earth did he pack?*

Owen took Scotty's bag and headed inside. Three long strides put distance between us. The farther he walked, the heavier the ache in my chest grew. Would he always be walking away?

Once we got checked in and inside the room, the boys helped bathe Destiny. She barely stirred, too tired to play with the bubbles. Her head bobbed forward, heavy with sleep. I knelt beside the tub, eyes closed, breathing in lavender soap, hoping the water would still be warm enough for me later.

Ten minutes. That was all she lasted. Winnie-the-Pooh pajamas on, she curled beneath the covers. "Hey, Mama, can we?" She closed her eyes and signed the word "Pray."

I knelt, resting my forehead against the burgundy bedspread—stained with the ghosts of a hundred strangers. *Lord, please let this have been washed this decade.*

Destiny patted my shoulder. The cue to begin. She folded her hands over her belly and whispered the prayer Michael and I had taught them long ago. "Dear God…Thank you for the day gone by…Thank you for the starry sky…Thank you for a time to rest…" She yawned. "Tomorrow, help me do my best…" Her breathing slowed. Sleep claimed her before the end.

I finished the prayer in a whisper. "Please give me joy and peace and love."

Her mouth moved softly, like a baby nursing. I tucked her hands under the blanket.

Joy. Peace. Love. All buried with my husband.

The room hummed and rattled. Air conditioner shaking in the window, neon vacancy sign flashing through yellowed sheers, rusted curtain rod sagging. A cracked mirror wore a Band-Aid like an apology. The carpet's original color was anyone's guess.

Scotty sat on a blanket between the dresser and the bed, his device glowing against his face. Two red scratches marked his cheek. His glasses slid down his nose, he pushed them back absently, and turned the page.

"What're you reading?" I asked.

"Braveheart," he whispered.

"For fun?"

He shrugged. "It was free." Scotty rubbed his eyes—the way Michael used to. "And I like it."

Suddenly, I realized one of my children was missing. I sat up and switched on the light next to the bed. "Where on earth is your brother?"

"Out. Said he needed air."

I stared at the window as headlights flashed past. "Did he say where he was going?"

Scotty shrugged and kept his eyes on his electronic book.

"How long has he been gone?"

"I don't know."

I grabbed my purse. My phone. My keys—

gone. "Did he take the car?"

Scotty sighed and set the device aside. "Mom… this is between you and Owen."

Before I could answer, the sound of a card key slid into the lock.

We both turned toward the door.

Chapter 8

Owen glanced at us as he walked in. "What?" The door clicked shut behind him.

"Hush. Your sister's asleep."

He whispered back. "Sorry, I asked."

My weariness had been replaced by anger. I jumped up from the bed and stepped in front of him, glared into his face, eight inches higher than mine. "Where've you been?"

He dangled car keys in front of me. "Drinking and driving. As small as this ungodly place is, I destroyed the entire town in less than fifteen minutes."

"You're disgusting," I said, snatching the keys from his hand and tossing them onto the dresser. Metal slid across fake wood and bumped against the TV. Destiny rolled over.

Owen placed his index finger against his lips and stared at me with a mocking grin.

I pointed to the exit. "Outside. Now," I said, resisting the urge to smack the grin off his face.

He pitched a paper bag to his brother. "It's all yours if I don't come back alive," Owen said, then opened the door and stormed outside.

With several deep breaths, I paced the width of the grim hallway before addressing my son. "What was so important that you left without telling me? You can't just sneak off when you want to. No more secrets, remember?" I folded my arms across my chest and waited for Owen to raise his eyes from the stain he stared at on the ragged carpet.

When he didn't answer, I took a step closer to him. "I can't handle more bad choices. Not here. Not now."

There. What plagued me so many times over the last few months, I finally said.

Memories of poor decisions, police cars, and crowded courtrooms crowded my thoughts. All without Michael. Owen refused to talk about what happened other than that he'd gotten involved with the wrong people and made a bad choice. Cocaine and gangs, in my mind, went beyond a bad choice.

Owen shifted one shoulder against the wall and crossed his arms. He rested one foot over the other, allowing the toe of his shoe to point into the worn green carpet. His eyes raised to meet mine. "Did it ever occur to you that we might still be hungry? But it seems like the only person you ever think about is your precious princess." Owen turned and opened the door. He hesitated with his hand on the knob. "Thanks for trusting me."

Before I could answer, the door closed behind him and left me to wonder if another one slammed shut on our relationship.

Back against the wall, I slid to the floor and fixed my gaze on the ceiling light.

"Where are you, God? Michael—how do I keep from losing Owen?" The same questions I'd asked for months whispered again. I didn't expect answers.

I don't know how long I sat there before another guest appeared. A woman in a tacky gray suit, peep-toed heels revealing red toenails that matched her long fingernails. A black designer knock-off purse hung from one shoulder. A small beat-up suitcase rolled behind her. She slowed, then awkwardly shifted her cheap purse away from me as she passed.

Her bottle-chestnut hair flipped at her thin neck. She nervously pushed her bangs aside and glanced my way.

I pointed to my hotel door. "Sleeping kids."

The cheap-looking stranger nodded and looked ahead again. Five doors down, she slid in a key card. Before disappearing inside, she glanced my way once more.

I shook my head. *What did she see?* An African American woman sitting in a hallway. Disheveled. Hair unsure whether it wanted to be straight or curly. Tear-streaked cheeks. A shirt still damp from bathing a special-needs child.

What she didn't see were three children torn from the only home they knew, still aching from their father's death. The weight of grief. The uncertainty of what came next. An unwelcoming father-in-law waiting at the edge of our future.

She didn't see one child who hated me, one I worried I couldn't protect, and one who clung to me because I was all she had left. And the one person I needed most, the man who stood beside me, lived life with me, was gone.

A paper sleeve with a room key inside lay beside me, slipped under the door. My way back in.

Fear of falling asleep in the hallway pushed me to my feet. I reentered the room quietly. The bathroom light spilled softly into the dark. The smell of French fries lingered. A crushed fast-food bag leaned against the trash can. On the dresser, a wrapped burger waited. *For me?*

I carried my bag into the bathroom. The tub still held water, cold now, the bubbles long gone, only a faint trace of lavender left behind—a wasted bath.

I drained the tub, pulled on one of Michael's old T-shirts and a pair of shorts, washed my face, and left the bathroom light on in case Destiny woke. In the other bed, Owen rested on his side away from me. I wanted to run my fingers through his loose curls like when he was younger, and I kissed the top of his head. His bare shoulders moved slightly with his breathing.

"I'm sorry," I whispered and crawled beneath the bedspread beside Destiny.

"So am I," Owen answered.

I tried settling in for the night, but sensed my son and I weren't apologizing for the same thing. *God, please give me joy, peace, and love.*

Morning arrived with Destiny rubbing my left cheek. I blinked, her face too close, and stretched against the knot in my back. "Good morning, Princess."

She pointed at the dresser.

"What?"

She pressed into my side and pointed again, signing for food. She'd spotted the wrapped burger still sitting there.

"The burger? No, sweetheart. Hold on."

I slid off the bed, careful not to wake the boys, and pulled dried apples from the snack bag.

Destiny pouted, glanced once more at the burger, then accepted the fruit. "Thank you, Mama. Do you want some, O?"

I swiveled and noticed Owen sitting in the shadows. "Have you been up a while?" I asked as I turned down the air conditioner. The ancient unit sputtered, whined, then settled into a low hum.

"Long enough." He drummed his fingers on the table. His beard was trimmed, hair still damp from a shower I hadn't heard. The faint scent of his cologne—Love and Luck—hung in the air.

"I'm sorry about last night."

"You already said that."

"Not to your face." When I rested my hand on his forearm, the drumming stopped. "I shouldn't have said what I did. Please forgive me?"

"Yeah, it's whatever."

"Thank you. And thanks for getting food. What do I owe you?"

"A little trust." He pulled away.

"Fair." I shifted. "Think you could make another food run? Breakfast this time."

"Who's paying?" A hint of a smile crept in.

I reached for my purse. "Debit card. Get what everyone will eat. Be sure to get apple juice for Destiny. And a large coffee and breakfast sandwich for me."

"Only one coffee?"

"For now." I stretched and rubbed the back of my neck. "Before you leave, please get rid of that burger because we don't want your sister to—"

"Yum," Destiny said through a mouthful of cold burger. A streak of ketchup lingered on her chin.

"Oh, Princess."

Owen laughed and slipped the card from my fingers. "I'll be right back with breakfast."

Scotty sat up, rubbing his face. "If you're taking orders—"

"Text me." Owen grabbed the keys and left.

Joy and peace and love.

For now, one was enough.

Peace.

Chapter 9

By eight, the SUV was packed, and we were back on the road. Destiny sat between Owen and Scotty, giving them extra legroom and keeping her from the door—only four hours to Gabe's.

Gabe was an early riser when he needed to be. At fifty-five, he'd told me have-to-be's were rare. A quick voice-to-text seemed easier: *Leaving Columbia at 8. Four hours away. Stops included. ETA ~1. Coming hungry. Eb.*

Sunday morning traffic on I-70 was light. I scrolled through the radio for a Christian station until a man with a heavy Southern drawl greeted me with, "Good morning, Columbia Saints."

Destiny clapped at the opening drums. "Turn up, Mama!" She nodded to the beat, then tossed her head back for the chorus she knew by heart. "God is in control." Her small fingers pointed skyward, echoing the words to hold on, not to be afraid.

Memories surfaced with the song. Michael's hidden dimples, his green eyes, his laugh lines deepening as we aged. Kitchen dances, his voice off-key but joyful. The smell of him, sweat mingling with freshly cut grass. And the ache, the bony hand, the weakened body, the final goodbye.

Owen and Scotty stared out their windows, lost in their own worlds.

When the song ended, Destiny patted my headrest. "Again, Mama."

"Princess, that was the radio."

"May I have my music?"

Her headset, relocated to my purse after last night's hunt, was handed over. The boys pulled out theirs, too. I turned off the radio, and we drove in quiet for hours, stopping for bathroom breaks to give Destiny time.

With just over an hour to go, we paused to stretch. Festus—a name that means joyful, and it showed. The town revealed itself in quaint black-and-white awnings, vertical neon signs, sandwich boards advertising specials, and small parks. Charming, welcoming, and fleetingly peaceful in the wake of our long drive.

We headed through downtown Festus to Shropshire Park. The playground carried the most important piece of equipment for Destiny—a swing.

As soon as I killed the engine, Destiny tried to crawl over Owen to get out. He gripped her shoulders. "Wait."

Once he unbuckled and exited, Destiny pushed him against the car door as she hurried toward the playground. "Be careful and remember your manners," he said as he watched her climb the stairs to a slide.

Scotty made his way to the back of the SUV and found the basketball. He headed toward the courts. "You coming?" he called over his shoulder to his brother.

"I guess." Owen ran to the court.

I sank onto a wooden bench behind the swing set, shoulders tight, letting the sun hit my face. Destiny pumped the chains with soft squeaks, swinging higher with every push. I dialed Gabe.

"I'm up," I said.

"Finally." His voice sounded raw from sleep.

"We're in Festus, about an hour from Cape Girardeau," I told him.

He coughed. "Why Festus?"

"Michael and I used to stop here. Kids could play before the drive. Beats an hour of, 'Are we there yet?'"

Destiny leapt off the swing, squatted in the sand, completely absorbed. I watched her little fingers trace shapes, the way she always noticed the smallest things.

"Is that girl still up at dawn?" Gabe asked.

"Not today. Last night wore her out." I let my gaze drift toward Owen, blocking one of Scotty's shots, rebounding the ball with quiet intensity. "They've all changed... especially Owen."

"Grief," Gabe said softly. "Everyone handles it differently."

Destiny crept toward me, a ladybug resting on her fingertip. She held it out. "You keep it."

The tiny creature crawled onto my leg, wings twitching, then rose into the air as Destiny skipped back to the swing.

I refocused on Gabe. "Is your stew still available?"

"Yeah. Bring the kids hungry."

"Thanks," I whispered.

"Don't thank me until you've had my beef stew. See you soon."

The line clicked. I watched Destiny swing as the wind lifted her hair. I thought of the children's prayer, joy, peace, and love.

For a heartbeat, I imagined Michael beside me. And for a heartbeat, maybe God had granted a sliver of joy, hidden in a small town called Festus, amid swing chains, sand, and the soft thrum of hope.

Chapter 10

The warm fall sun had lifted our spirits so much that we were all reluctant to get back into the vehicle.

Destiny buckled herself in the middle seat and huffed. "Are we almost there?"

"Almost," I said as my sons slid in on either side of her, still perspiring after their basketball game, filling the car with a combination of sweat and body spray.

Destiny glanced at each brother and scrunched her nose. "How far is almost?"

Scotty used the bottom of his sweatshirt to wipe sweat from his face. "Closer than not yet."

"And further than 'round the corner," Owen said, and rubbed his cheek against his shirt, leaving a large wet spot on the shoulder.

The boys leaned forward, sharing a quiet grin over a memory of their dad. I turned away, letting them hold it a moment.

"Are we there yet?" Destiny's small voice broke the silence.

"Soon, Princess."

"It'd be faster if I drove," Owen muttered.

"I'm fine," I said. "Thanks for offering."

The last stretch passed in drowsy quiet. Destiny slept before Bloomsdale. Scotty and Owen followed soon after.

Scotty stirred as we exited Interstate 55. I peered at him through the rearview mirror. I saw that his eyes were fixed on the Cape

Memorial Park Cemetery. The white stone entrance and the weeping willow made him still, silent, watching until it faded behind us.

Boulder Crest Drive curved into Hunters Lane. The tension in my chest eased as the woods closed around us. The dirt road rocked the SUV gently, sun catching small treasures in the soil. Gabe's tractor had smoothed the worst bumps, but the drive still demanded attention.

White gravel led to Gabe's house, perched on stilts, half log cabin, half treehouse, hidden beneath the hill. Memories tugged at me. Michael had carved our initials here after we married. Each son's name had followed. Destiny would've had hers carved this year. I prayed she'd forgotten.

The house itself was nearly unchanged. Wide stairs led to an A-frame porch with six rocking chairs and honey-colored rails. New wildflowers softened the edges, a touch of life Gabe hadn't bothered with before.

Gabe stepped onto the porch, jeans, work boots, plaid shirt open over a black tee. His cap was in his hand. "Where are the troops?" he called, his voice carrying over the driveway.

"They're still waking up," I said and walked toward him.

Scotty exited the car, stretched, and waved. "Hey, what's up!"

"Festus works wonders," Gabe said as he jogged to us and embraced us in a giant group hug.

"That and a little too much heat," I added, as I pulled away and examined my brother-in-law's kind, tired face.

Owen appeared, shielding his eyes.

"Great beard," Gabe said as he threw an arm around his nephew's shoulder.

Owen pointed to his uncle's head. "What happened to your hair?"

Gabe rubbed his newly shaved head that now made his salt-and-pepper beard stand out more. Dark brown eyes that seemed too old for fifty-five, mapping the loss and labor of years.

I stared up at him, aching at his uncanny resemblance to Michael. "You didn't tell me about the haircut."

"Everyone grieves differently, Eb," he said, voice low, full of unspoken sorrow. Lines etched across his forehead and mouth, the roadmaps of a man who had weathered life and loss.

Gabe pulled them in for another group hug. I let the hug linger. For the first time since Michael's death, I felt the fragile thrum of hope—and the ache that it might never be enough.

"Uncle Gabe!" Destiny ran from the SUV.

We moved aside as she leapt toward him.

Her uncle lifted her into the air, gave her a squeeze, then placed Destiny on her feet. He knelt on one knee in front of her.

She rubbed his head. "I like it."

He chuckled. "Glad you do. How's my little Squirt?"

Destiny straightened. "I'm not a little Squirt anymore. I'm Destiny. I'm all grown up."

"That's right. Your Mama told me that."

She rested her hands on his chest. "She told you about me growing up?"

My brother-in-law gazed at me over Destiny's head. "Something like that."

"Where's Kid?" she said, searching for Gabe's overweight, arthritic bulldog.

"Kid is probably in the backyard doing something he shouldn't. Why don't you go find him?"

"Okay." Destiny rubbed her hand over Gabe's head as she walked past him.

"Hey, old man, where should I put our bags?"

Gabe took a few bags from Owen's shoulder. "Better watch your mouth. I've still got a couple of inches *and* muscles on you."

Owen nodded toward the house. "Same place?"

"Loft's ready."

Owen nodded and headed to the house.

Scotty trailed behind, staggering under the weight of his bag. "You're not old."

"Hey, Owen. Hear that?" He wrapped his arm around Scotty's neck. "You should learn from your brother here."

"Yeah. Right," Owen said before disappearing through the front doors.

Scotty wrestled free of his uncle's arm and hurried to the open door. "I've got to claim a bed before Owen does.

"Take your time," Gabe said. "I switched the mattresses. You'll end up with the better one."

"Good looking out," Scotty said as he jogged the rest of the way to the house.

Gabe turned to me and flashed a white smile. "Every now and then, got to play a little favoritism to my only namesake," he said, referencing Scotty's full name, David Scott McMullen, which was a combination of Gabriel and Michael's middle names. Gabe headed to the open trunk, grabbed a bag, and held up my blue duffel. "Yours?"

I nodded.

He closed the trunk, and we headed to the house.

I held onto his arm. "Gabe, please don't take this the wrong way, but don't let Owen hear you say you favor Scotty. We've had enough conflict already between the—"

"A little rivalry might distract them," Gabe said.

"Not sure that approach helps," I replied, suddenly feeling exhausted.

He led me to the stairs. "Sit. There are worse alternatives."

I reclined against a cedar beam and stared at Gabe. "Meaning?"

A flicker of something, concern, maybe worry, crossed his face. "Never mind all that. Let's talk about you for once, Eb." Gabe coughed. "Be honest. How're you doing?"

I blinked back tears, unable to answer at first. My chest tightened, and I wondered if I'd ever be okay again. "I'm...not doing well." I fought back against my first impulse, which would have been to run to the nearest bathroom, my latest form of cost-effective therapy.

"Come here," he said, and gently pulled me to him like a father with a small child. "Let it out, Eb. Don't hold it in. It'll kill you." Gabe allowed me to literally cry on his broad shoulder. We stayed there several moments, until something broke inside of me. I sensed a release

I hadn't experienced since Michael's death. Gabe patted my back until the sobs lessened.

"I'm ready to go inside," I said and wiped my face with my sleeve.

"Let's do it," Gabe replied, then guided me upstairs and opened the front door.

The rich, savory smell of stew hit me first. "Hmm," my stomach rumbled.

The kids had already claimed the kitchen. Destiny perched at the table with a glass of milk, while the boys rummaged through Gabe's cabinets for bowls.

"Glad y'all made yourselves at home," Gabe said, nudging me closer. "Hope there's enough left for your mom and me."

Owen ladled stew into a large bowl and smirked. "Maybe," he said and handed me the bowl.

Destiny scooted in close. "I saved you a seat, Mama."

The warmth of family, imperfect, fractured, yet present, filled the room. For a moment, the grief, the exhaustion, and the long journey faded.

Outside, the afternoon sunlight slanted across Gabe's porch, casting long shadows on the driveway. Tomorrow would bring questions, challenges, and the unknown that waited beyond these walls. For now, the children's laughter and the aroma of stew were enough. But even in that comfort, a quiet tension lingered, whispering that the road ahead was far from over.

Chapter 11

After lunch, Gabe and I sat on the back deck while Destiny curled up in the hammock with her arms wrapped around her ladybug pillow. As she rocked, her sweet voice sang herself to sleep.

Owen and Scotty grabbed fishing poles and a tackle box from the storage beneath the deck and made their way to the pond. Scotty pointed across the glass-like surface to where a ripple spread across the water. His brother walked past him to the end of the dock, shielded his eyes, and looked in the direction of the disturbance. He set the tackle box down and both searched for the perfect lure.

Adjusting the zero-gravity lounge chair, I reached down to scratch Kid's head as he reclined between Gabe and me. Kid rolled onto his side in my direction, his back leg lifted, his way of asking for a belly rub. Although, his wide girth prevented him from resting his leg in any other position.

"You need to put Kid on a diet."

As if he understood, the aged bulldog gave a low growl.

Gabe stretched, rested his head on the back of the chair, and intertwined his fingers together over his chest.

"We're two happy bachelors, why spoil a good thing?"

Kid, having endured enough scratching, rolled onto his belly and huffed. Before long, he was snoring.

"Can I ask you something?"

Gabe frowned. "No promise I'll have the answer."

"Why'd you leave?"

He turned his head in my direction. "I'm assuming you mean North Carolina?"

I nodded.

"Well, it was time."

"What do you mean?"

His attention shifted toward his nephews fishing on the dock. "My father and I didn't see eye to eye. By the time I was Scotty's age, I was Owen's size and five inches taller than my dad." He turned to me. "Can you imagine trying to deal with a rebellious teen who towers over you?"

"I think I can imagine that."

"Sorry. Guess you can." Gabe chuckled. "Michael inherited the Irish McMullen look. Green eyes, red hair. I took after Mother's family, stocky and dark-haired. Maybe I reminded my father more of his wife than he wanted to be reminded."

I stared at him and nodded. Gabe towered at six-five, a full five inches taller than his younger brother. They shared the same thick, wavy curls—Michael's rust-colored, Gabe's dark as night.

"At eighteen, I'd had enough of being second best to the perfect child. Michael was only four when I left, but by then I knew what my father thought of him . . . and me."

"How so?" I asked and drew my knees up from the sunlight creeping onto the end of the chair.

"I wanted to go to college, engineering, or something. Always had a love for tinkering with stuff, especially trucks. He wanted me to stay and help run the hardware store. I didn't have the best grades, mainly because I didn't try, but I applied to colleges and universities anyway."

"By yourself?"

He nodded. "I even paid the application fees myself. I got accepted to a small school not too far from home. Catawba College. What I didn't know at the time is that they didn't have what I was looking for, but so what? What mattered was that they'd sent me an acceptance letter."

"I never heard you mention this before. Did Michael know?"

"Never told him."

"Why?"

"I didn't see the need to do so."

"Hey, Mom," Scotty shouted from the dock. He raised his pole, and a small fish dangled on his line.

"Nice work, but that's a runt," Gabe said. "Throw him back and catch something we can cook for dinner."

"You got it." Scotty removed the fish from his hook and tossed it back into the pond.

Gabe leaned back. "After high school, Pops said we couldn't afford college. My grades didn't help, and sports weren't enough to get a scout. So, I worked in the store until I could pay my own way."

He swatted at a fly. "One July day, I was in the stockroom doing inventory. Michael was playing with tools. A customer came in, and Pops started bragging about sending Michael to college. I stepped out. Pops turned, saw me, shut up. That apron he forced me to wear, I slammed it on the counter, left the store, and was gone before he got home." He paused. "Time for a real drink. Want one?"

"No thanks. I'll have a diet soda please."

"Wimp," he said, letting his hand rest on my shoulder before heading inside.

When Gabe returned, Owen was on the deck eyeing his uncle's drink. "Beer. Cool."

"Only if you're twenty-one," Gabe said, handing me a soda.

Owen leaned against the railing. "Couldn't you just give me one?"

"Absolutely not, Owen." I took a gulp of my drink.

"You heard your mother." Gabe straddled the lounge chair again, popped the top, and nodded toward the fridge inside. "Water and sodas are in there."

Owen mumbled something under his breath as he got two sodas and walked toward the pier.

I rested a finger on my ice-cold soda. "May I ask something?"

"Sure, if I haven't bored you yet."

"Have you ever been interested in marriage?"

Gabe rubbed his shaved head. "With this mug, who'd have me? My only kid," he pointed to his dog sprawled under the hammock, "is that bulldog."

"Give me a real answer."

"Okay, real answer." Gabe reclined, gazing at the sky. "Alice. Marie. Spencer. McMullen."

"But that's your mom—"

He held up a hand. "Yep. I'm going somewhere with this. I promise."

"I think you're avoiding the question."

"Just listen," Gabe said. "My mom was incredible. I lived fourteen years under her roof before realizing how good life had been. She died giving birth to Michael. The bachelor life was mine after that."

I sat up and crossed my arms. "I've always hated hearing about your mother dying so young, but I'm still not seeing the correlation."

Gabe gave a crooked half smile and lifted one shoulder. "It correlates. Trust me."

"It's a sad story, but I'm not buying it as an explanation. Sorry."

He studied the amber in his glass for a moment before answering. When he spoke, his voice was easy, but quieter.

"When my mom died, my dad didn't just get sad. He… came apart. The whole house felt like it'd lost gravity. One day, everything's normal. Dinner, laughter, my mom humming while she washes dishes. And the next day it's like somebody pulled the center out of the room."

"That must've been hard."

He rolled the glass between his palms. "It was. I watched a grown man who could fix anything suddenly not be able to fix himself. Couldn't sleep, couldn't eat, couldn't even walk into their bedroom for months. Love did that to him." He glanced up with a small shrug. "Hard lesson for a kid."

"That's your logic?" I asked.

"It's not logic," he said lightly. "It's instinct. You see what loving someone that deeply can cost, and a part of you starts thinking maybe it's safer not to gamble the whole house."

He took a long swig from his drink, then pushed himself to his feet and pointed toward the hammock. Destiny had climbed down and was now sprawled beside Kid, her arm draped over him, her ladybug pillow tucked under her head.

"You okay with her cuddling with her cousin?"

"As long as he doesn't drool on her."

Right on cue, Kid lifted his head, a long strand of drool hanging from his jowls.

Chapter 12

Once the sun chased the shadows from the deck, I slipped inside to my room—Gabe's room, though it felt different now. Before Michael died, he always insisted that his brother and I take the large bedroom with its oversized rustic furniture, while he bunked with Owen and Scotty in the loft. Destiny had her space across from the master suite. Her spacious retreat was a quiet refuge from her brothers.

When the boys were small, pillow fights ruled their bedtime. Gabe igniting them at night, the boys carrying the chaos into the wee hours of the morning. As we all grew older, the fights faded, leaving only echoes. Gabe's rituals remained, a quiet rhythm during our visits, but the laughter had shifted. Now, Owen and Scotty murmured their gentle complaints about Gabe's snoring, a faint reminder of nights filled with joy and of Michael, whose absence made even familiar sounds seem hollow.

Through the window, I watched Destiny try to get Kid to fetch. She held one of his toys over her head, a tennis ball on a string, and flung it across the yard.

I laughed when Kid looked up at her, sat, and dropped to his belly at her feet. He stood when she ran across the yard to retrieve the toy, then she repeat the process. So did Kid.

Destiny is going to sleep well come bedtime.

I searched for the boys and watched as Gabe walked over and stood on the dock with his nephews. No words appeared to pass between them, yet they all seemed content in the silence.

For the moment, contentment came in the quietness of the house. Thankful for the downtime, I nestled between pillows against the headboard with a fourth cushion on my lap as a desk. *Here goes.* I pulled Michael's thick, worn journal from my bag and held it to my chest before opening it.

My fingers traced the beautifully inscribed words, and I inhaled deeply, taking in the delicate aroma of aged paper and Michael's cologne. There were parts of his writing I could recite by heart, but the sight of his penmanship never grew old. He varied his writing style between cursive, print, and a mix of the two. It was as if he were several different men wrapped up into one incredible being. Studying the combination of cursive and print as they flowed across the tattered pages made me feel closer to my husband. It was as if he lived between the handwritten pages, and I could meet with him there. Again. And. Again.

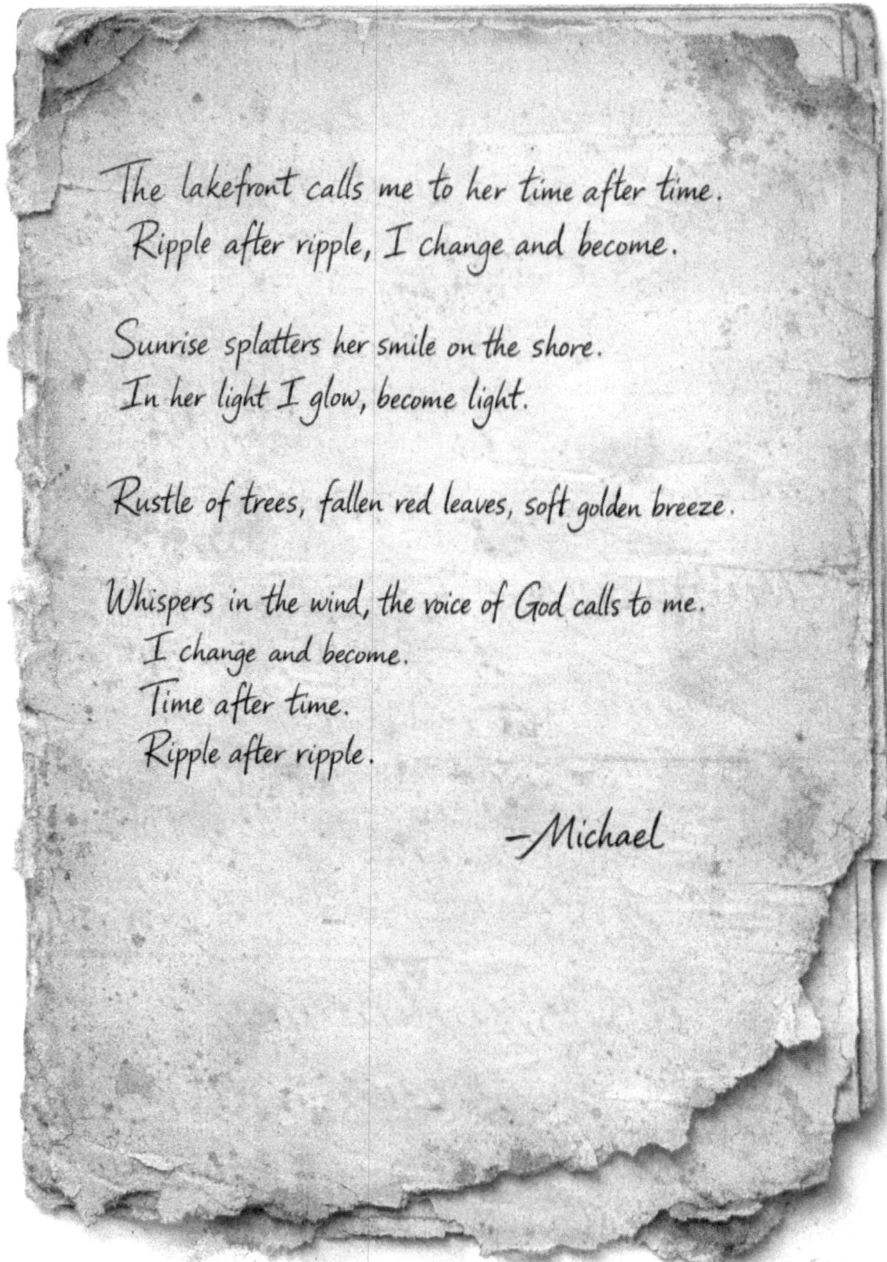
The lakefront calls me to her time after time.
Ripple after ripple, I change and become.

Sunrise splatters her smile on the shore.
In her light I glow, become light.

Rustle of trees, fallen red leaves, soft golden breeze.

Whispers in the wind, the voice of God calls to me.
I change and become.
Time after time.
Ripple after ripple.

—Michael

I was halfway through one of his poems when there was a soft knock on the door. Instinctively, I closed the journal and tucked it under my thigh. "Come in."

"Am I interrupting anything?" Scotty asked as he poked his head through the door.

"Not at all," I lied. "What's going on?"

He sat on the side of the bed closest to me. "Uncle Gabe is having a talk with Owen."

"How do you know?"

"He told me I could play video games." Scotty ran a hand through his hair. "Downstairs."

"In his theater room?"

Scotty's eyes brightened. "Yeah, that's exactly where he said I could hang out. By myself."

I beamed watching my son's animated face, knowing the basement of Gabe's home was every man's dream come true. It was complete with a theater-sized screen used for special occasions, or in this case, to ensure privacy. "Do you remember how everything works?"

Scotty nodded, stood, and walked to the door. "I just wanted to make sure it was cool with you. That's all."

"Be careful with your uncle's stuff," I called after him. Alone again, I peered out the window. Owen and Gabe sat at the end of the dock with their feet dangling over the water. *What're they discussing?* A throb of pain jolted me back to reality, and I sensed my face flushing. *Michael should be the one on the pier with our son.*

I wiped my face and shoved Michael's beloved journal in my bag. I placed the bag between the pillows and, for the first time in days, fell into a deep, dreamless sleep.

The hammock's sway woke me first. Startled, I reached for something to steady myself when I looked around, noticing I was still in Gabe's bed. Then I realized why. Destiny had climbed into the bed. She'd been pressing her knees into my back, nudging me gently but insistently. Soft kisses landed on my cheek, warm against my cool skin.

I rolled over and hugged her. "Okay, you win." I kissed the top of her head.

She giggled, smelling faintly of dog. Her bright eyes met mine.

"Have you been loving on Kid?"

"A little."

"Where's everybody?"

"Getting ready."

"For what?"

Destiny pushed up and bounced on her knees as she announced. "Pizza and Tunes at Twilight."

Tunes at Twilight was an outdoor event in Old Town. And one of the activities we always did as a family with Gabe when we visited. With blankets and picnic dinners, we'd listened to one of the local bands.

No. Please. Lord, I can't do this without Michael. "How long did I sleep?"

"Long enough for Uncle Gabe to order pizza." Destiny hopped off the bed and skipped out of the room.

A quick trip to the bathroom revealed my bedhead and the imprint of a pillow sham's edge, leaving a crease along my jawline. The time on the deck had added redness to my brown cheeks. The sleeves of my blouse pushed up, revealing varying shades after my time in the sun. I finger-combed my flattened curls and dabbed my face with a towel to take off some of the shine. The eyeliner and mascara, I'd applied hours earlier, were still presentable. "This is as good as it gets."

I followed the echoes of laughter and the tantalizing smell of garlic and Italian herbs coming from the kitchen.

When I entered, Gabe held up a slice and took a bite. "Sorry. Eb, we decided not to wait."

"I noticed," I said, walking by, two large pizza boxes on the counter next to him.

"It's really good, Mom," Scotty said with a mouthful of the delicious-looking pizza.

"And it's still hot," Owen added.

"Did you eat it all?" I asked, staring at what appeared to be empty pizza boxes.

"Yes." Gabe held his half-eaten slice toward me. "Want a bite?"

"Really?"

Scotty was the first to laugh, followed by the others. He removed a third box from the oven and placed the pizza on the counter. "We didn't want you eating a cold dinner."

The aroma of baked dough, onions, pepperoni, and sausage wafted through the air. I pulled a slice from the box, making sure to get all the dangling strings of cheese before narrowing my eyes at Gabe. "You guys ate two large pizzas?"

Destiny patted her stomach. "I helped."

"If I hadn't ordered three, leftover stew would've been your dinner," Gabe said.

"What about Tunes at Twilight?" Scotty asked.

I shook my head. "You guys go. I'll stay here."

Gabe arched a brow. "Why?"

When I didn't respond, he stepped in front of me, blocking my view of the kids. "It'll be good." Gabe leaned in. "For all of you."

The dough seemed to expand in my mouth. "I'm not ready."

"If you don't make up your mind, you'll never be ready."

"Hey, is that entire box for Mom?" Owen stood from the table with his empty plate.

Gabe placed his hand on the lid. "The rest of this one's for the park. Get ready, we're leaving in a few minutes."

His words earned a questioning look from me.

"We're *all* going," my stubborn brother-in-law said.

Destiny stared at the bulldog. "Even Mama and Kid?"

"Yep."

The sleeping dog jumped to his feet and barked.

One slice of pizza was all I could finish.

Chapter 13

The pizza box warmed my lap as we drove into town in Gabe's Jeep. Blankets, folding chairs, snacks, and my three kids crowded the backseat.

Gabe cranked the ignition, and country music blasted.

Owen and Scotty groaned.

"You kids don't appreciate good music," Gabe said, steering down the long, tree-lined driveway.

Both boys slipped in earbuds. Gabe lowered the volume but didn't surrender. "In my day, we all listened to the same station. When the radio worked, we listened to Pops' choice."

Destiny shook her head. "No, thank you. Mama, music please."

I dug beneath the pizza box for her headphones. Gabe smirked and switched the station to classical.

Sunlight filtered through the trees' canopy, shadows dancing across the dirt road. Sparrows flitted between cedar branches. For a moment, I wondered if they stayed together for life.

"I really hate talking to myself," Gabe said. "Especially when I thought I had company."

"Sorry."

Destiny hummed behind me.

Gabe hesitated. "About tonight. The boys told me that on the way down here, Destiny—"

"She's still afraid of the dark," I finished. "There's still plenty of time before sunset, and besides, the concert's only an hour."

He squeezed my arm but said nothing more.

Old Town came into view. Broadway. Annie Laurie Antiques. Lace curtains framed the windows. Even from the street, I could smell lemonade and fresh chocolate-chip cookies. Michael used to groan when I dragged him inside, but he always came. We once found Destiny's christening gown there. Years later, the ladybug pillow she refused to sleep without. How I missed the way he'd smile and say, "I like the company."

"My grief lies all within," Gabe recited suddenly, "and these outward shows are shadows of the unseen sorrow."

I stared at him.

"Shakespeare," he said. "Last girlfriend was a theater actress. Drama queen in every sense."

"What does that have to do with anything?"

"Don't mistake grief for defiance, Eb." He turned onto Lorimier Street.

"Everyone else gets grace for their grief," I said. "Why do I have to hold everything together?"

"Who said you have to?"

"Uncle Gabe! We're here!"

Destiny slapped the back of my seat. The band's warm-up music drifted through the open windows. But no one heard the grief crying inside me.

Once we set up our chairs and spread the blankets, the boys grabbed pizza and a basketball and headed for the court. I sank into a folding chair. Gabe shortened Kid's leash and sat beside me.

Destiny clasped her hands in front of her uncle. "Can I walk, Kid?"

"Do you think you can handle him?"

"I'm a big girl now."

Gabe looked at me.

Destiny climbed onto my lap and pressed her cheek to mine. "Mama, please."

I searched Gabe's eyes, silently asking him to go with her.

"You need to let her go," he said softly.

"Daddy will be with me," Destiny whispered.

The words knocked the air from my lungs.

"Okay," I managed. "Walk in front of us where we can see you."

Gabe secured the leash around her waist with a carabiner. "Don't lose my child," he teased.

Destiny smiled. "Come on, Kid."

The bulldog lumbered forward.

Gabe nodded toward a small concession stand across the quad. "Bo's Best. The owner spoils Kid with vanilla ice-cream. They'll be fine."

I watched until Destiny and the dog stopped at a sign reading "Doggie Break." The vendor handed her a spoon. She laughed as Kid waited patiently.

Gabe cracked open a soda. "May I be frank?"

"Aren't you always?"

"I can tell you've got reservations about moving Home."

"I do. Pops hasn't exactly forgiven me for marrying his son and us moving to Colorado."

He shrugged. "He's never liked me either. But I think the move will be good for Pops and your family. Especially Owen."

"Why's that?

"Because of the trouble he got into." Gabe chugged his drink.

My jaw tightened. "You mean about how he didn't know he was transporting drugs? Or how the judge suggested we leave the state after he was granted immunity?"

"Ebony, I didn't mean anything by—"

"He quit his job without telling me. Transported drugs for his so-called friends, who told him he'd make some quick money. And he never saw a problem with that? He didn't ask what he was delivering. Why didn't he talk to me? Why keep it secret? I hired an attorney I couldn't afford *and* prepared to sell our house to avoid foreclosure."

"He told me he was trying to help, Eb." Gabe shook his head. "Well, now you have the family home."

Gabe shook his head. "In the meantime, my father held onto the family home, hoping Michael would recover."

"Thank God, because it's the only place we have left." I scanned the quad.

The basketball thudded in the distance. The band launched into their first song. Families filled the lawn. But I didn't see a little girl with a bulldog. My chest tightened. "Where's Destiny?"

Chapter 14

Kid waddled toward us with his leash dragging the ground. He no longer pulled my daughter.

The crowd had grown from a small cluster of family and friends into a wall-to-wall sea of picnic baskets, multicolored blankets, and coolers stretching all the way to the bandstand.

But no Destiny.

"Gabe! Where is she?"

Turned in a circle twice but couldn't locate her.

His chair toppled as he launched toward Kid. He swore. "Didn't I tell you not to lose my niece?" He yanked the leash hard enough to cause Kid to yip. Gabe righted his chair, tied the leash around the leg, then pointed a finger in Kid's face. "Stay."

Kid crawled under the chair.

The crowd swallowed Gabe as he moved in the direction we'd last seen Destiny. Even at a run, keeping up with him took effort.

"Bob, have you seen my niece?" Gabe's booming voice exploded above the growing noise.

Bob placed a scoop of vanilla ice cream on a cone. "Do you mean that colored girl who was walking your dog?" He handed the treat to a waiting customer.

Did he just say "colored?"

"That's my daughter you're referring to," I said as I tried to slow my rising frustration and anger by taking a deep breath.

Bob adjusted his sailor's hat and pointed his ice-cream scooper at me. "What's your point, girl? I'm just stating the obvious facts."

I shook my head and stormed away from Bob, who couldn't have been much older than sixty but used words I thought we'd moved past.

I heard Gabe shouting at the ice-cream salesman in the background as I put as much distance between myself and people like Bob.

"What's wrong with you?" Gabe barked. "What'd you call my sister-in-law a girl and my niece colored for?"

I was out of earshot to be able to hear Bob's response. The crowd became a blur of faces. None of them hers. "Princess, where are you?" My words were more prayer than question.

On stage, one of the mikes shrilled causing me to cover my ears.

"Sorry, folks, too much amp." Tall, thin, and with a ponytail hanging down his back, the guitarist chuckled.

I continued searching the crowd for brown curls, bright eyes, the way she tilted her head when she smiled. My little girl with the extra chromosome. My little girl who trusted everyone. My little girl who stood out in every room she entered.

"Destiny!" I screamed. "Princess!"

The band's microphone shrieked, then instruments exploded into song. The sound swallowed my voice whole.

I ran toward the stage, waving, desperate for the mic. If she heard her name, she'd come. She always came.

The guitarist winked at me.

I balled my fists and ran to the stage. Rage flared. Hot, useless, and dangerous.

Gabe grabbed me from behind and hauled me back. "What're you doing?"

"She needs to hear me!"

"Bob thinks she went behind the bandstand. The boys are looking."

"You said let her go!" I shoved against him. "Are you happy now?"

Fear sharpened into accusation before I could stop it. "Michael would never have let her go alone!" I shouted, my finger in his face.

The pain in Gabe's eyes cut through me. But my inner terror drowned everything else. Because my child wasn't just missing. She was small. She was different. She was vulnerable. She was biracial in a town that still used words like *colored*. And I wasn't there to protect her from the unthinkable.

The world narrowed to worst-case images. Someone leading her away with a smile. Someone noticing her innocence. Someone deciding she was an easy target. I'd seen the news reports and the statistics about girls just like Destiny who never saw their families again.

I couldn't breathe.

Then Owen appeared at the edge of the crowd.

He stepped aside.

Scotty followed, Destiny, resting against his shoulder, her arms looped around his neck, as if nothing had happened.

My knees gave out before I reached them.

Scotty lowered my daughter into my arms, and I collapsed onto the grass, sobs ripping from somewhere primal and ancient. Not caring who stared and judged.

Destiny patted my hair, seemingly confused by the magnitude of the entire situation. "Don't cry, Mama. I'm okay." She pressed her mouth close to my ear. "Daddy was with me. He showed me a ladybug. Then Bobo found me."

My heart cracked wide open.

"Daddy doesn't want you sad," she said, cupping my face in her warm hands. "Everything's going to be alright."

Behind us, Gabe stood still. Not angry. Just older somehow. "I need a beer," he muttered.

"Me too," Owen added.

Gabe shot me a look. "Better with me than some punk kid."

Too tired to argue, I watched as they walked off together. Same height, same stride, grief stitched into both their backs.

Scotty lingered. "Mom?" His hand rested lightly on my shoulder.

I looked up at him. Michael's half-smile stared back at me.

"I'm sorry," I whispered. *For yelling. For unraveling. For dragging you all back to a town that could swallow us whole.*

He didn't ask what I meant. He just turned and followed the only men he had left.

And I held my daughter tighter, knowing fear had just shown me how quickly everything else could disappear.

Chapter 15

After the concert, Gabe laughed with the boys, clapped shoulders, and swapped stories with locals as if nothing had happened. He never looked at me.

Later, awkward tension followed us home. In the Jeep, country music blared again. Louder than before. No one argued.

Destiny fell asleep before we reached the dirt road exiting the park.

Once home, I tucked my daughter in early, her lashes resting soft against her cheeks, then I went looking for Gabe.

He was on the porch, alone, in the rocker. A pipe rested in his hand, unlit at first. He struck a match without looking up. Smoke curled between us, thick and sweet.

I leaned against the rail. "Do you have anything you want to say?"

"Nothing you'd want to hear." He drew a plume of smoke in, held it, and let it drift out slowly.

"Sorry, would be nice."

"I'm sorry." The evening light caught the smoke but did nothing to soften Gabe's grim expression when he stared back at me.

"It's just that Michael would've —"

He held up his pipe like a stop sign. "Enough Michael. Is. Dead." Each word landed like a hammer. "Not in Colorado. Not in Carolina. Not anywhere." He swore under his breath. "And I'm not him."

I straightened, thinking of what to say next.

"I watched my dad wait for my mother to walk back through the door," he went on. "Hospital must've made a mistake, he said. She's not dead."

"I know that must've been so difficult for you," I said, wishing I could remember everything I had planned to say.

Gabe took another pull on his pipe. "For days, he relived it. Then months. When he finally accepted that she wasn't ever coming back, he poured everything into Michael. You'd think he'd resent the child who cost him his wife." A hollow laugh. "But no, instead he worshiped Michael."

Smoke drifted toward the dark trees.

"A part of him died when he let her go. That's when he let go of me."

Silence stretched thin between us.

He looked at me then—really looked. "Are you doing that?"

I folded my arms tight across my chest, a shield more than a posture. "I'm not your father."

Gabe studied me as if debating what to say next. "No, you're not Shane McMullen. You're Owen's mother."

He went inside before I could answer.

I gripped the porch rail until the wood pressed crescents into my palms. *He has no right. I'm Owen's mother. I was the one who sat in the courtroom. I signed the papers. I mortgaged what was left of our life. I stood between my son and the world when it turned on him.* And still, I was the one being accused of letting go.

"Mom?"

Scotty's voice cracked on the single word.

I pulled in a breath and turned. "Hey, son."

He stepped beside me at the rail. Taller than I remembered. Shadows carved angles into his face that the moonlight couldn't soften.

"You, okay?" He frowned. "I came out here to make sure you and Uncle Gabe were okay. Sounded like you two were arguing."

I stared at him, realizing that he was so much like his father it hurt. "I will be." I slipped my arm through his.

"We could stay a few more days," he said. Casual. Careful. "If you want." On the edge of manhood. A faint shadow darkened his lip. He was trying to be steady for me.

"You'd like that wouldn't you?"

"I wanted to catch a bigger fish than Owen." He smiled, but it stopped short of his eyes.

"Maybe next time. But I really think we need to get going." I leaned closer. "Are you okay with that?"

"I guess."

"Is there something else on your mind?"

"It's just that all my friends are in Colorado. I miss them. And I miss…" His gaze drifted past me, somewhere into the dark. Then he straightened. "But it's okay, Mom. We'll be fine."

I tightened my grip on his arm and stared into the night, wondering if either of us believed it. "Yeah, we'll be just fine."

Our words hovered between us like something fragile—beautiful and easily broken.

Chapter 16

The next morning, Gabe made pancakes. He always did on departure day.

I packed slowly, folding and refolding shirts that didn't need it. If I lingered long enough, maybe breakfast and Gabe would be over.

Laughter drifted down the hall. My stomach betrayed me first. When I stepped into the kitchen, Destiny launched from her chair and wrapped herself around my waist. "Morning, Princess."

She beamed up at me. "Bobo beat O."

I looked to the table.

Scotty patted his stomach. "Twenty-one all gone." A proud grin.

"Pancakes?" I asked.

"That's right," he said.

Owen shoved back his chair. "Figured I'd let him win at something."

"It was close, though. How many did you eat?" Gabe flipped three golden pancakes onto a plate without looking up.

Owen grinned. "Nineteen." He stood. "If you're packed, Mom, I'll load the car. The rest is in the foyer."

I blinked. "You're… loading the car?"

Destiny wiggled free. "I want to help!"

"I'll get my stuff," Scotty said, already moving.

The kitchen emptied in a rush of sneakers and screen doors.

"Don't look so shocked, Eb. They're good kids. All of them are." Gabe held out a mug. "Drink."

I took the large mug and inhaled. Hazelnut. Strong. Familiar. "What'd you do to Owen, you didn't give him any of that beer he's been hinting at, did you?"

"No, I put him to work." Gabe pulled out a chair and motioned for me to sit. "At the park, I handed him the truck keys and told him to move it closer to the pavilion. Then I had him help haul the grill and coolers. Figured if he's going to stand around looking like the man of the house, he might as well practice being one."

He reached for the syrup and poured it high over my pancakes, the amber stream falling in a slow ribbon.

Michael used to do that.

He'd hold the bottle over the boys' heads like he was testing gravity, a sticky waterfall that ended in baths and shrieking laughter. Destiny would clap like it was the best magic trick in the world.

My throat tightened.

"I didn't traumatize the kid," Gabe muttered, misreading my silence. "Eat."

I cut into the pancakes. Warm fruit burst across my tongue. "What's in these?"

"Apricots. Squirt wanted peaches. Closest thing I had."

Of course, he'd had apricots. Of course, he'd used them.

I ate like I hadn't in days.

For a minute, there was only the scrape of forks and the quiet hum of the dishwasher. Then Gabe said casually, "Bob's old school."

My fork stopped halfway to my mouth. "Colored," I said.

He didn't flinch. "Deep South. Small town. Like me."

"We're in the twenty-first century," I said. "Has anyone told him?"

"Doggonit, Eb." His voice sharpened. "You're heading to small-town Carolina. It's even more country than where I live. I didn't see a Black person in Home until I was a teenager. Places like this don't rush to change. You've got to understand that."

I set my fork down. "Understand?" I let out a short laugh. "Gabe, understanding isn't the problem."

He frowned slightly.

"You're talking about a town being slow to change," I said. "I'm talking about living inside the reason it needs to."

The words hung between us for a few seconds.

"I've spent my whole life learning how to read a room before anyone says anything," I continued quietly. "Knowing which smiles mean welcome and which ones mean tolerate. Knowing how long I can stand somewhere before someone starts wondering why."

Gabe shifted in his chair.

"That kind of understanding doesn't come from growing up in a small town," I said. "It comes from growing up Black."

Silence settled over the table.

The pancakes suddenly felt heavy in my stomach.

"Anyway," I said, picking up the mug and washing the bite down with coffee, "the car's probably packed by now."

"Maybe you and your family can be the change Pops needs."

"I'm not here to make people comfortable with who I am." I set the mug down harder than I meant to.

"It's just that—"

"Mama! Come look!" Destiny said as she burst through the door. She tugged my arm toward the porch.

I put my mug down and followed.

Outside, she was already halfway down the steps. "Here!"

Owen sat in the grass near one of the support beams, tossing a knife into the dirt, catching it, repeating. All of their initials were carved deep into the wood from years ago.

Beneath them, fresh, raw against the grain, new letters.

D.M.M. for Destiny Marie McMullen.

"Owen remembered!" she squealed, throwing her arms around his neck.

"Easy, Desi." He laughed. "I need oxygen."

I stepped closer and ran my fingers over the new cuts. Then over Scotty's. Owen's. Mine. Michael's, older now, weathered but still there. A record of who we had been in this place.

"Thank you, Owen," I said softly.

He stood, brushing grass from his jeans. "Someone had to do it." He headed for the SUV. "I'm riding shotgun this time."

"You can't," Scotty called. "What about the TV?"

"Uncle and I rearranged everything. It's in the back."

Gabe nudged me toward the driveway, his hand light against my elbow.

"I still don't like how fast this is all happening," he said quietly. "But Home… that part I do agree with."

He glanced back at the house. At the carved posts. At my boys loading the last bags into the car while Destiny climbed into the backseat with Lady B tucked under her arm. His mouth curved into a small smile, but something in his eyes stayed distant, like he was measuring more than the moment.

"Is that right?" I asked, still angry from our earlier conversation.

"I've been telling you," he said. "That place has a way of pulling people back." He let his gaze linger on the property a second longer than felt natural, then looked down at me again. "You'll see soon enough," he said, his voice softened.

"I'll see what?"

"There's no place like Home."

Chapter 17

Gabe hugged each of us before we left. When he held me, he didn't let go right away. "Stop pushing people away," he said quietly.

Owen drove first, taking us into Kentucky. Scotty rode shotgun. Destiny and I sat in the back, boxed in by everything we owned. I tried to wrap an arm around her, but the seat belts and the tight space made it impossible. Boxes groaned behind Owen as he shoved his seat back for more legroom.

At the first gas stop, the boys switched places. Owen didn't ask to drive again.

Eight hours carried us through Kentucky, Tennessee, and across the line into North Carolina. When the state sign appeared, Gabe's words looped in my mind.

"Stop pushing people away."

We stopped for lunch at All Souls Pizza in Asheville. It was hard to say what the kids enjoyed more, the pizza, the horseshoes out back, or simply being free of the SUV.

The last stretch of road felt different. No one slept. Destiny hummed and tapped Lady B against her lap. Scotty read. Owen stared out the window as if memorizing what we were leaving behind.

"Are we driving through Welcome?" Owen asked.

Every visit, Michael had gone a few miles out of the way to pass through Welcome, North Carolina. He told the same joke every time.

"What's the use in going to Home without a welcome?"

We would pile out of the car and take a picture by the Welcome sign. Then we would take another when we reached Home. Later, Michael would splice them together, so the photos read "Welcome Home." One year, he tried to skip it, thinking the kids were tired of the tradition. They made him turn around.

"You can't break tradition," they told him. *But what was the use of those traditions now that Michael was gone?*

"We could stay on 52 and cut across," I said as we approached Bethesda.

"So, no stopping at Welcome?" Owen asked. "Dad would've stopped if he were here."

My hands tightened on the wheel.

"Mom, I want to stop," Scotty said softly.

Destiny clapped her hands. "If you're happy and you know it…"

The tension cracked.

We pulled into the lot beside the small country store. Owen went inside first. The rest of us stretched beneath the fading afternoon sun.

The Wilsons had owned the store for decades. Rod had built it onto their house after growing tired of strangers knocking on their door asking if Miss Loretta had something good to eat. He always told the story the same way. People would walk for miles for her pies, fried chicken, and biscuits. It fed their eight children and kept him happy.

Owen emerged with a dark-skinned, stately-looking older gentleman at his side.

Rod was smaller than I remembered, heavier too. His limp was worse. He rocked from side to side as he walked, swinging his right foot forward. At eighty-five, he still refused to retire. "Sorry for your loss, Miss Ebony," he said, pulling the pipe from his mouth. "Hate to hear these things. I'm so grateful you stopped by."

"We had to. It's a family tradition."

"Loretta would come out to greet you, but her knees are actin' up. Storm's coming." He looked up at the sky. "You'd better come inside before the rain comes. We've got cold drinks and fresh fried pies. Apple and sweet potato."

Michael loved those pies. "We'll be right there, but we need to take a few pictures first."

"Of course," he said and blew a small ring of tobacco smoke. "I'll take them for you."

We lined up by the Welcome sign. Michael's spot stood empty. The absence pressed against us as Rod took several pictures.

Inside, Loretta rocked in the corner, her curly gray hair pulled into a messy bun. The chair creaked in a steady rhythm. She looked up over her wire-rimmed glasses and put aside a blanket she'd been crocheting. "Ebony, come here, honey."

Her hug smelled of nutmeg and wood smoke. Tears came before I could stop them.

"I prayed the Lord would heal him," she said. "Even in pain, we trust Him. We're y'all heading?"

"We're moving to Home."

"That sounds like a fine plan." Loretta nodded and pushed her glasses back. "You need family. Even more so than ever."

"True." *If she only knew.*

"But remember that family ain't always blood," she said, as if reading my mind. "I've thought of you as family since you were carrying your first baby." Her eyes drifted to Destiny. "She's still your little baby, huh?"

I nodded.

"Destiny is a pretty little girl. I can tell she's special."

I frowned, wondering where Loretta was going.

"I ain't blind." She held up her hand. "I know she's got Down syndrome. But don't ever let anyone tell you that she ain't something real special. God's hand is on her strongly. Pay attention to that and don't ever underestimate the power of her calling."

"Thank you. I've always sensed that, and you confirming it," I said as my voice cracked. "Makes it that more real."

"I got something else to tell you." Loretta patted the stool beside her, indicating that she wanted me to sit down beside her.

I sat and waited.

Loretta leaned over and rested her arm in my lap. "I've been trying to tell Mr. Wilson to lose some weight," she whispered. "But, I realized that I hurt his feelings. So, guess what I did?"

"What?" I asked, enjoying the moment.

"I just moved the buttons on all his overalls instead." Her smooth brown skin crinkled into a bright smile as she watched her husband with my children. "Sometimes love means adjusting things quietly."

I followed Loretta's gaze across the store, where the boys sampled beef jerky. Destiny clutched a honey bear and stared at Owen until he sighed and pulled out his wallet.

"Fine young men," Loretta said. Her gaze settled on Owen. "And don't worry about the oldest. Keep praying more than worrying."

I raised an eyebrow. "Why'd you say that?"

"It's the way you look at him. I can tell you're worried."

"Is it that obvious?"

Loretta chuckled and patted my hand. "I'm a mother too and with all those kids and grands, you know, *I know*."

"I'm sure you've got all types of wisdom from raising a big family."

"My wisdom came at a tough price way before I ever became a mother."

"Really, how so?" I asked, my eyes wandering over the intricate crochet pattern of the blanket in Loretta's lap.

She tucked the crochet needles into a colorful ball of yarn and sat up. "My mama died young. She'd had two babies in two years. The third came while she was fading away in her bed. And those times, we were too far from the hospital to get help in time. When we laid that baby on her chest, she said he had the lungs of his father. Two days later, she was gone."

"I'm so sorry."

"Mama never saw us grow up. But we kept her here." She tapped her temple first, then her chest. "We keep each other alive in the telling. The remembering hurts at first. One day, the stories give back more than they take."

I swallowed. "Thank you, that's a beautiful way of looking at a hard situation."

She nodded and continued to pat my hand. "Love doesn't die when the body does," Loretta said. She pointed to my temple, then my chest. "Michael's story may have ended on Earth. But his legacy continues through his family. You just have to trust yourself to keep him alive in the telling, remembering, and allowing his story to give back."

Just then, Rod appeared with a grease-stained paper sack bulging with pies.

"I guess this is your cue to get back on the road again," Loretta said. "Thank goodness, y'all don't have much further to go."

"I know, but leaving is always so hard." I leaned down to give her one last hug, and she pushed something into my hand. When I opened my palm, a lustrous pearl lay in it.

"When I heard the news about Michael, I knew I'd give this to you whenever I saw you again."

The jewel glistened as I examined it, realizing it'd been part of a necklace. "It's gorgeous. But you really don't have to—"

"God put it on my heart to give it to you. It belonged to my Mama.

"Then there's no way I can take something so precious," I said and attempted to return the pearl.

Loretta closed my fingers around the gift. "Long ago, I dismantled my Mama's necklace, and I've given one pearl to a person who has suffered loss. This is the last one, and I wanted you to have it as a reminder that God uses symbols like a pearl to show us, he can take any horrible, uncomfortable tragedy and make something beautiful from it."

I nodded and secured the pearl into a compartment in my purse for safekeeping. "Thank you," I whispered and hugged my friend once more.

Back in the car, the air was filled with cinnamon and children chewing while discussing the things they'd gotten at the store.

"How many pies were in that bag?" I asked as I turned onto the highway.

"The better question is how many are left," Scotty said, handing one to me. "It's still warm."

The pie was solid and familiar in my hands, like a loving hug from Loretta. I checked the rearview mirror and watched my children laugh, sunlight catching their faces just right. For a moment, Michael was there. Not as a ghost. Not as a memory slipping away.

Just present.

I took a bite, savoring the buttery sweet potato filling, reached into the small compartment in my bag, and fingered the treasure Loretta had given me.

Hope felt resilient like the pearl, tasting like apple, sugar, and something that refused to die.

Chapter 18

We passed a faded sign, "Explore Home," indicating our entry into the small town. A large farm on our right had low-growing vegetation, likely tobacco, not ready for harvest. Open fields gave way to brick houses with long gravel driveways. Occasionally, a tire swung from a tree, and dogs rested on lawns needing rain.

A lone car approached from the opposite direction. The driver raised his fingers from the steering wheel without letting go as he passed us. Michael used to call it the Carolina wave. Total strangers greet when passing.

I returned the gesture.

The sharp curve in the road led us three miles downtown, to the location of the oldest building in town, Pop's Hardware Store, owned by Shane Owen McMullen, my father-in-law. Shane blamed me for Michael not returning to North Carolina to run the store, and though he never said it, he blamed me for his son's death. Across the street from the hardware shop was, Dee's Diner, the second oldest establishment in town.

"Mom, can we stop at the diner? I'm starving." Scotty held up an empty paper bag that once stored fried pies.

Destiny tapped my shoulder. When she caught my eye in the rearview mirror, she signed "milkshake."

I shook my head. "Okay, the diner it is," I said and parked in the diner's lot. Chairs and three small cast-iron tables lined the sidewalk.

Plastic lace tablecloths, anchored by legs, lifted in a light breeze, but couldn't escape. Red checkered curtains hung in the front windows. *Today's special—meatloaf,* was written on a dusty chalkboard.

The interior held gleaming chrome under fluorescent lights, red vinyl booths, black-and-white checkered flooring, and round cherry-red vinyl stools at the bar. Cracks in the vinyl showed age.

"Sit wherever y'all want." A waitress said while servicing another table. She wore a pink knee-length dress. Her brown hair pulled back in a ponytail, a few strands escaping to frame a young face that couldn't be more than nineteen, maybe twenty.

Destiny skipped to a booth next to a window and pushed the curtain back as she settled into her seat. I sat beside her, and Scotty sat opposite, grabbing a menu from the clip at the end of the table.

I spun around to see where Owen had gone and spotted him at the far end of the diner seated at the counter. "We're sitting over here. Come join us." When he didn't look up, I stood and walked to where he was. "Why are you sitting here?"

Owen continued staring at the screen above the grill. "The Tour de France is on. I wanted to watch it." He glanced back at his siblings, then continued staring at the screen. "Without *any* distractions. Like how dad and I used to do."

"Can't you see it from the table?"

"I just wanted a few minutes to myself, Mom." Owen kept his focus on the screen. "Is that too much to ask?"

I sighed and walked back to the two children who didn't mind having me as their mother. "Hey, I'm going to stop by Pop's to let him know we're here." "Order me a chocolate milkshake, along with your orders. Remember to get what you need, *not* what you want. That should be enough to cover it." I shoved some bills into Scotty's hand.

Scotty frowned. "Why don't we all go together after we're finished eating. We want to see our granddad too."

"Don't worry, you'll get a chance to see Pops. Just enjoy your food while I take care of grown-folks' business," I said before exiting the diner and walking to the hardware store. Two locals sat in rocking chairs in front of Pop's. They nodded, and I did as well.

As I entered, a bell jingled, and I was transported back in time. Straight ahead, between two aisles of old and new tools, sat an old-fashioned cash register on a worn wooden counter. A glass display beneath it held more items for purchase. As I walked to the counter, odors hit—fertilizer, cleaning supplies, and the faint mustiness of ancient inventory I couldn't imagine anyone needing.

Shane emerged from a door separating the business from his living quarters. He wiped his hands on a rag and tossed it next to the register before looking up. "I see y'all got in okay."

I stared at Michael's father, tracing the same green eyes. Only colder in the older man, like bullet-proof glass instead of grass. How could two men share a face and not a heart?

Shane stood slightly stooped over at seventy-nine, looking older than his age. Time had stripped him down but not softened him. What'd once been thick, red hair like Michael's was now white and thinning, clinging to his scalp in stubborn wisps. Age spots mapped his sagging cheeks like stains that wouldn't wash out. His body was narrow, almost gaunt against his five-foot-ten frame, as if bitterness had eaten what time had left behind.

Where Michael carried strength with steadiness, Shane wore his like a weapon. His jaw was sharp. His mouth permanently set in a line that suggested contempt was his resting state. Even standing still, he appeared confrontational, like a man who'd spent a lifetime hardening himself against a world he never tried to understand.

The resemblance was undeniable. The difference was immeasurable.

"Hello, Shane." My voice came out strained. "We just pulled in."

"Where are the kids?" He asked, his tone indifferent, as if "the kids" weren't his grandchildren.

I stared at the counter between us and swallowed. "Your grandkids are across the street having milkshakes at Dee's."

Shane picked up a nearby rag and wiped an already clean countertop. "The movers got to the house early this morning."

"Are you saying that—?"

"That your stuff is here," he said, and used the same rag to blow his nose. "Yeah, I figured you wouldn't mind me letting the movers in the house to unload."

"Not at all." I stared at the rag as Shane shoved it into his shirt's pocket. "Everything is inside, then?"

He nodded. "Everything's inside. But I don't know where you'll find room for all that stuff. The house ain't that big. The barn ain't neither."

"Thanks for letting them unload." I swallowed. "And thank you for the house. It means the world to—"

"Ain't no need to thank me." He pulled a toothpick from behind his ear and used it to poke between his front teeth. "I promised the house to *my* boy. And quite frankly, this is the closest I can come to giving it to him."

Shane let the toothpick hang from the corner of his mouth, studying me like a stranger who'd just stepped onto his property and had already disappointed him.

"Thanks again, Shane."

"Get your family settled. A storm's supposed to be coming in. Supposed to be a bad one." He dug in his pants pocket, retrieved a set of keys, and placed them on the counter. "Guess I won't be needing this no more."

"I've already got a set of keys. Go ahead and keep the ones you have in case of an emergency, and that way we can —"

"Won't be no need. For none of that." Shane pushed the keys in my direction and cleared his throat. "Ain't my house, now."

We stared at each other for several seconds before being interrupted by the brash ring of a telephone. "See you around, I've got to take that," he said and disappeared behind the door, leaving the chasm between us wider than it'd been before.

Alone, I stood there while my father-in-law barked into the phone. He tore into some poor clerk about a late delivery of batteries, as if the fate of the world hinged on double A's arriving on time. His voice was sharp, cutting through the empty store like a razor, each word dipped in irritation and superiority.

Before the person on speakerphone could finish a sentence, he ended the call with a string of curses.

For a moment, I thought of waiting for him to reappear so I could share all the things I'd ever wanted to say, but I didn't trust myself to speak.

I reached for the keys on the counter. The metal scraped against wood, loud in the charged air. Without looking back, I walked out and pulled the door shut behind me, hard enough for it to rattle in its frame, but not hard enough to give him the satisfaction of knowing he'd shaken me.

The two men slouched in their weathered rockers, paused mid-sentence, their conversation about some overstocked fishing pond stalling just long enough to size me up. One squinted. The other shifted tobacco from cheek to cheek. Then, as if I were nothing more than a passing truck, they eased back into talk of bait and water levels.

Through the diner window, Destiny caught my eye.

She waved.

A tall glass gleamed in her hand. She lifted it higher, nodding toward the pink milkshake swirling inside.

I waved as I walked to the diner.

Destiny spun around for several seconds and looked back at me. Her expression now dark, unsettled, unfamiliar. Her smile was gone.

Then she mouthed something I couldn't hear.

Chapter 19

I ran across the street, all the while my eyes locked on my daughter's worried face. The bell above the diner door hadn't finished ringing before I saw it. Splintered glass glittering under fluorescent lights, vanilla milkshake bleeding across black-and-white tile at Owen's feet.

Scotty was already up. He reached his brother first, hand firm on Owen's shoulder, whispering low and urgent.

Owen jerked away. His barstool screeched backward as he leaned toward the waitress. "Want to ask him the same thing?" He jabbed a thumb at Scotty.

The waitress clutched her order pad to her chest, lip trembling. A Coke float pooled beside the milkshake, brown foam creeping toward the grout, glass shards scattered like shrapnel.

I stepped carefully through the wreckage and stood beside Owen. "What happened?"

The waitress pointed a pen at Owen. "I didn't mean nothin' by what I said to him." Tears brimmed in the girl's eyes.

Turning to him, I crossed my arms. "Owen. Apologize."

"Of course, Mom." His laugh was sharp. "You don't even know what happened, but I did something, right?"

"Mom, please." Scotty moved between us. "You don't know the full story. It wasn't Owen's fault. I saw the whole thing—"

I held up my hand and turned to the waitress, reading her tag. "I'm sorry, Katy. I'm sure this was an accident."

"I know." She wiped her reddened face. "I knocked over the float."

Owen groaned.

"But I meant no harm, ma'am." Katy pushed an escaped lock of hair behind her ear. "I just hadn't seen y'all before. I've only been here a few weeks."

Owen left where he'd been at the counter and plopped down at the table across from Destiny. Scotty followed.

"I just asked him what he was." Katy sniffed and dabbed her forehead with a dish towel. "Didn't see no harm in that. He's got green eyes."

The air shifted.

Katy used the dish towel to swat at a fly.

"Is he? I mean, he isn't—"

"Black?" I asked, my arms crossed.

Color drained from her face. "I ain't never seen no Black person with green eyes." She hurried for the mop. "Anyway. When I asked, 'What are you?' he got mad. I got flustered and—" she gestured at the mess— "didn't mean any harm."

"When you asked my son, 'What are you?'" I took a deep breath. "What you really wanted to know was his ethnicity, right?"

"His eth— oh!" Her eyes widened as if the word itself had tripped her.

I stared at the young woman. *She had no idea. No idea she'd turned my son into a category. A curiosity. A specimen.*

The kitchen doors banged open.

"Katy! Orders in the window!" Delores Johnson filled the doorway. Nearly six feet of beehive blonde hair, flamingo lipstick, and authority.

Then she saw me.

"Ebony McMullen. Well, I do declare!" She ran to me and wrapped me in a hug that smelled like fried chicken and grease. "Had to finagle out of Shane when y'all were coming." She wiped her hands on her apron. "And the young'uns? Where they at?"

I nodded toward the table where my children sat.

"Lawd have mercy. Them ain't young'uns no more."

She turned on Katy. "How many is that now? Four glasses?"

"It was—"

"I know." She shook her head. "An accident. Next one's coming out your paycheck."

Katy fled.

Dee lowered her voice. "She's jittery. Not the brightest candle on the birthday cake, if you know what I mean. But she's a sweet girl. Little flighty."

Across the diner, Katy was already nervously giggling with new customers.

Dee nudged me. "And honey… those are some fine-looking young men."

Young men. The words landed heavier than the glass that'd broken. I stared at my friend, noticing the halo of silver roots jutting out of her red dye job. "To me, they're still my little boys, but the reality is Owen is nineteen, and Scotty's not too far behind."

"Got that right," Dee said and strode to the table. "Hi, family. How y'all doing?"

"I had two milkshakes." Ice cream circled Destiny's mouth. "Scotty told me I could have Mama's after the lady broke the glass." She beamed and sat back.

Dee laughed and pinched Destiny's cheek before turning to the boys. "Gentlemen." She shook Scotty's hand. Then Owen's. She didn't let go right away. "You outta school yet, Owen?"

My son didn't try to pull away. He held Dee's gaze. "Yes, ma'am."

"Need a job?"

He pulled away. "Depends on what it is."

"Well, I'm losing my morning' dishwasher."

Owen looked at the ceiling fan and sighed.

I fought the urge to kick him under the table, but I said nothing.

Dee continued as if she didn't notice his disrespect. "Full time, more than minimum wage." She leaned toward him, placing her palms on the table. "And I feed you. Want it?"

"Maybe." He folded his arms and stared at her.

"Good, I'll give you two days to help your Mama get settled. I'll see you at 5:30 Wednesday morning." She gathered the empty glasses and turned away before Owen could respond.

He arched his brow at his brother. "Did she say a.m.?"

Scotty laughed.

"Too much of a good thing." Destiny moaned and patted her stomach.

The low rumble of thunder was the first sign of an approaching storm. Bright sunlight gave way to shade; a gust of wind rattled the window.

I peeked through the curtains and frowned. "Time to go if we want to beat this rain." Our chairs scraped against the floor during my search for the bill I'd asked for earlier.

"If you're looking for the bill." Scotty handed Destiny a napkin. "Ms. Dee took it when she grabbed the glasses."

When I got to the register, I gestured to Katy, who'd just finished giving a departing customer change. "Our bill, please."

She shook her head, streaks of crimson dotting her cheeks. "Ms. Dee said no charge."

"No. Let me pay." I pulled out my wallet.

"But Ms. Dee—"

"Ebony." Dee motioned from the kitchen door.

Next to the cash register, I placed a five-dollar bill.

Katy shook her head. "But Ms. Dee said that you didn't have to pay for—"

"I know." I lifted my index finger. "This is a tip for you."

"You didn't have to do that, ma'am." Her eyes never met mine. "Especially after that, um, misunderstanding.

I turned to Dee who pretended to be wiping the counter. "Now, look, you know I always pay my way no matter —"

"Not this time, sugar," Dee said, motioning for me to come closer. "Got a welcome home gift for you."

Destiny jumped up and down. "I love gifts! Can I have one too?"

"You sure can, hon." Dee smiled softly. "This kind of gift is meant for all of y'all."

She bent behind the counter and came up with an oversized paper bag, pressing it into my arms. The weight knocked me off balance. A gallon jug followed. I nearly dropped it, but Owen stepped in, taking the tea. Scotty lifted the bag from me without a word.

"I won't talk about what happened to Michael," Dee said quietly. "I've always hated sympathy. Just never know what to say." She patted the bag. "So, I help with what I can in the way I can. Meatloaf. All the fixings. Sweet tea. Packed enough for five."

Five?

We were four.

"Dee, we don't need—"

"Oh, honey." Her hand settled on my shoulder. "Those boys will take care of any leftovers. Figured I'd pack extra."

My throat closed. "I can't thank you enough."

Thunder cracked overhead, closer this time. The windows rattled.

"You'd better git going." Dee turned me toward the door and gave a gentle shove. "Owen, help your mama. And don't forget. This Wednesday morning, you start your new job."

Another boom shook the diner.

And the lights flickered as we exited Dee's Diner.

Chapter 20

The speed limit read thirty-five. The storm behind us moved faster. In the side mirror, a gray wall stitched sky to ground, swallowing the horizon. I pressed the gas. Fifty. Fifty-five. "Lord, just let us get there safely," I whispered as I drove.

The SUV fishtailed into the gravel drive at 1465 Morning Glory Road.

The house waited.

White paint peeled in thin curls from the clapboard siding. The porch sagged slightly at the left corner, wind chimes twitching in warning. Black shutters hung unevenly beside tall windows that reflected the bruised sky. The roof dipped in the middle like a tired back. Home. Or what was left of it.

"Everybody out!" I shouted before bolting from the car.

Fat drops splattered my arm the second the door opened, cold, sudden. Lightning ripped across the sky.

Destiny tilted her face upward. "Cheese!"

Thunder cracked overhead.

I grabbed her wrist and ran. Gravel found its way into my shoes. The porch boards groaned beneath us. "Keys, keys, keys—"

My purse swallowed my hand whole.

Destiny reached into my jacket pocket. The spare set Shane had insisted I carry spilled into her palm.

"Thanks, Princess."

The door stuck before giving way. The smell hit first. Closed-up air. Old wood. Lemon oil. A faint trace of something sweet, lavender sachets, maybe, buried in drawers decades ago.

We stumbled inside as the wind shoved against the door. Scotty followed, juggling the food. The storm struck full force. Oak branches thrashed against the house. Chimes clanged like warning bells. A gust blasted through before I could slam the door, spraying rain across the narrow entry. Water hammered the tin edge of the roof like thrown pebbles.

For a moment, I just stood there. This was Michael's childhood home. The hardwood floors were narrower planks than we'd had in our Colorado home, scarred, uneven. The living room ceiling sat lower than I remembered. A brick fireplace leaned slightly off-center. The wallpaper along the hallway peeled at the seams, faded roses the color of old blush.

Our former house had been open and bright and new, granite counters, high ceilings, rooms that echoed with possibility. This one felt smaller. Closer. Like it had been holding its breath.

Boxes towered everywhere, labeled in thick black marker. KITCHEN. MICHAEL'S BOOKS. WINTER CLOTHES. FRAGILE. Lamps leaned against armchairs wrapped in plastic. The couch barely fit the space. Every object we owned sat in cardboard, waiting to be placed. Waiting for decisions. Waiting for me. My chest tightened. At least there was a roof. At least there were walls. At least my children had somewhere to sleep tonight. Relief slid in quietly, almost guiltily.

"Where's Owen?" I shouted over the storm.

Scotty shrugged, rain dripping down his face.

I flung the front door open and leaned into the downpour. The driveway was empty. I shut it hard and pressed my back against it. "Scotty. Where's your brother?"

"I don't know." He peeled off his soaked shirt. "I'm his brother, not his keeper." He grabbed the food and disappeared into the galley kitchen, smaller than the one I'd once ruled, its linoleum cracked near the sink, cabinets painted a yellow that had faded into buttercream.

"Mom," Scotty said. He stood at the nook window.

"What is it?" I asked.

He pointed at what he'd been looking at. Through sheets of rain, red taillights glowed inside the old barn-garage. Owen sat in the driver's seat.

"You found him."

"You're welcome," he said in the same clipped tone his brother had perfected and walked away.

The taillights blurred. And so did my vision. When the storm softened to steady rain and my tears finally thinned, I stepped back into the living room. Scotty sat beside an open box, clean shirt on, cap low. Destiny splashed in the puddle near the door, shaking water off Lady B.

"We match!" she announced, spinning to show her soaked pants.

I twisted, feeling the wet fabric clinging to my skin. Cold. Heavy. *Why not?*

I stepped into the puddle with her.

We jumped. Water splashed the scuffed baseboards. She squealed, stomping harder. For a moment, the house sounded alive.

The door flew open.

Owen nearly collided with us, sunlight breaking around his shoulders. "Thought you'd want to see this." He set the gallon of tea down and stepped back outside.

Destiny darted after him.

As I followed behind her, I touched Scotty's shoulder. "I'm sorry."

He held my gaze, then nodded once.

I took a deep breath. Outside, the air was clean, smelling of oak and wet earth. Broken twigs littered the yard. Sunlight struck the dripping leaves. Destiny stood between her brothers, pointing upward. "A promise, Mama!"

I looked up. Two rainbows arched across the sky, clear, complete, impossibly bright against the retreating storm. All the colors. Every single one. "Wow." The word barely formed.

"A picture, O!" Destiny tugged his hand. "Before the promise is gone!" She reached for me.

I hesitated, thinking of everything broken, everything missing, everything still in boxes inside that too-small house.

Scotty nudged me forward.

We gathered, wet, disheveled, arms around one another. Owen held up his phone. *Click.* The image froze us in time.

Owen rested his forearm on my shoulder. "Left me out in the storm, huh?" he said before he flicked Scotty's cap and bolted across the yard.

Scotty tackled him. They crashed into mud, wrestling, laughing, real laughter this time.

No photo captured that. But I felt it. The house behind us stood quiet, older, and imperfect. But ours. And for the first time since Michael's funeral, I allowed myself to believe that maybe we would survive here.

A crack split the air.

Not thunder.

Wood.

All four of us spun around.

The sagging porch beam shifted.

And the front corner of the roof dipped, just slightly, before settling into something that didn't look steady at all.

Chapter 21

Wednesday morning arrived before the house was ready for it. The air still carried the scent of cardboard and dust from two straight days of unpacking. I stood at the edge of the kitchen, stifling a yawn, watching Owen's silhouette framed by the refrigerator light. "Want me to take you?" I asked.

He popped up from the fridge, water bottle in hand, startled to see me awake. "Isn't this a little early for you?"

Five-ten. Even the sun hadn't committed yet.

He closed the refrigerator and glanced down the hallway.

"They'll stay asleep. If Destiny wakes up and doesn't see me, she'll crawl into Scotty's bed."

He drank half the bottle in one pull, then wiped his mouth with the back of his hand. "Bike's ready. Means of transportation for now, so I might as well get used to it."

The words *for now* lingered between us.

"Good luck on your first day," I said as he reached for the door.

"Yeah. As a dishwasher."

"A paid one," I reminded him gently. "You've had practice."

He smirked. "Maybe I'll work my way up to cook. Chores covered that, too."

Before he could shrug me off, I stepped forward and wrapped my arms around his waist. For a second—just a second—he held me back.

"Gotta go, Mom."

The porch light flickered against the dark sky. No hint of dawn. He strapped on his helmet, the small beam of his bike light cutting a narrow path down Morning Glory Road. I watched until the faint whir of tires gave way to frogs croaking in the distance.

Everything in me wanted to grab the keys and follow. To trail him at a distance. To make sure no one stopped him. No one questioned him. No one saw only what they expected to see. But the safety net had been torn months ago. The lies, drugs, and arrest had shattered something fragile between us. Trust didn't rebuild overnight.

I closed the door and leaned against it.

The house answered with silence.

A small lamp in the corner pushed back the darkness. Most of the boxes were gone now. A few remained stacked near the wall, waiting for decisions I wasn't ready to make. Our Colorado couch sat awkwardly between two-barrel chairs Shane had left behind. New and old pressed together without harmony. Granite counters traded for laminate. High ceilings gave way to low ones that held the warmth close. Function over beauty. Survival over style.

I curled my knees beneath me and studied the framed photograph on the end table. Michael's remission dinner. His favorite steakhouse. The mechanical bull outside. The old photo booth just past the hostess stand.

"We're celebrating," he'd said, tugging us toward it. "We need proof."

The boys wore cowboy hats too big for their heads. Destiny and I had tied red bandanas around our necks. Michael stood in the center, smiling at the camera. Crow's feet deepened around his green eyes. Six years of cancer had thinned him, dulled his red hair with threads of gray, but he was still there. Still ours.

That strip of glossy paper had frozen the last uncomplicated joy we would ever share. Months later, our family numbered four.

"Mama?" Destiny shuffled into the room, blanket dragging behind her, curls wild from sleep. She climbed onto the couch and pressed a finger against the glass. "Morning, Dad," she whispered, hugging the frame.

I brushed her curls from her forehead and kissed her temple. "Why are you up?"

"I woke up." A yawn swallowed the rest.

"O's gone?" she asked.

"Yes."

She studied my face for a long moment, then placed her small palm against my cheek. "He's okay, Mama." Her warmth steadied me in a way I didn't want to need.

"What woke you?" I asked softly.

"Daddy."

Every muscle in my body tensed.

"He said you needed me."

Michael is dead. The words echoed Gabe's voice from days ago, firm, unyielding. Not in Colorado. Not in Carolina. Not anywhere. I swallowed. Had I missed something again? Was grief finding a new way to speak through my children?

"Baby," I said carefully, pulling the blanket higher around her shoulders. "Daddy is gone. You know that, right?"

She inhaled slowly, then let it out without answering.

"Destiny, we need to talk about…"

Her breathing evened out. When I looked at her, she was snoring softly.

Smiling, I eased the frame from her limp fingers and held her against me. The house creaked softly as if adjusting to our weight, to our sorrow. Outside, the first hint of pink edged the horizon.

I must've drifted off, because the next sound tore through the room like a siren.

"Mom!" Scotty barreled in, phone clutched in his hand, face drained of color. "Owen's at the police station."

The photograph slipped from my lap and hit the floor face down.

Chapter 22

I fired questions at Scotty like bullets. "Where is he? What happened? Why would they?"

"I don't know." Over and over. Same answer. Same tight jaw.

I ran for my room and threw on an outfit from the hamper—something I'd worn the day before.

At the front door, Scotty caught my arm. "Mom. Your purse."

I pivoted back.

"And keys." He held them up.

I grabbed them, breath shallow.

On the porch, he stopped me again. "Please don't forget to keep your phone nearby."

"I will," I said, my stomach tightening. My mistake earlier. I hadn't answered. That's why Owen called Scotty. I snatched Scotty's baseball cap off his head and jammed it over my uncombed curls. No mirror. No makeup. I swiped my tongue across my teeth. Please let there be mints in my purse.

The key missed the ignition twice before sliding home. *Owen's at the police station.* Words that should never belong in the same sentence. Anger burned hot and directionless at him, at this move, at the fact I didn't even know where the police station was. Somewhere off Main. There shouldn't be a need to know. Not in a new state. Not again. Not with the same child.

The sun hovered low, dew still clinging to the roadside grass. The air smelled of damp earth and diesel. Two chickens darted across the road, feathers flashing white. I slammed the brakes. Less than two hours ago, I'd hugged him, told him to have a good first day at work. How had it unraveled so fast?

Dee's Diner, where Owen should've been, was dark inside. The CLOSED sign swinging slightly in the window. I turned onto Main and prayed.

Four blocks later, a red brick building came into view. HOME POLICE STATION.

I parked crooked beside a patrol car and ran up the steps. The building smelled of old coffee and lemon disinfectant. My pulse thudded in my ears.

Inside, a woman sat behind a small desk, elbow propped, chin resting on interlaced fingers. Black-rimmed glasses with a silver chain. Perfect lipstick. Country music hummed low from a radio. "Yes?" One brow lifted.

"I'm looking for my son."

"Name?"

"Owen McMullen."

A door opened in the nearby hall.

"You're such an idiot."

Dee's voice.

She stepped out of an office, filling the hallway with floral perfume and power.

Owen followed behind her. Hands in pockets. Head down.

I shook my head. *Déjà vu.*

He looked at me, his jaw clenched.

I looked at Dee. "And what has my son done now?"

"Owen?" She snorted. "Nothing. Hank's the complete idiot."

Confusion tangled with the anger in my chest. "What happened?"

"What happened was the local deputy didn't recognize him," Dee said. "They saw him riding his bike before sunrise. Asked where he was headed." She stuck a piece of gum in her mouth and chewed. "When he told him he was working at the diner and Hank found it still closed, he brought him in to 'straighten things out.'"

From inside the office, a male voice muttered, "Sorry, Aunt Dee."

"No specials for you this week, Hank," Dee shot back.

She turned to me. "The station called me when he couldn't reach you."

"I didn't have my phone on." The words tasted like failure. "Owen, I'm so sorry to have—"

"It's fine." He wouldn't look at me. "Everything is straightened out now."

"Overzealous nephew of mine," Dee said under her breath. "Good cop. Most days." She patted Owen on the shoulder. "You still up to working, sugar?"

"Yeah." Owen's voice was flat. "It's not like I'm needed anywhere else."

"Good. Grab your bike. I'll give you a lift."

He passed me.

I reached for him.

He stepped away.

"Eb, darling." Dee guided me toward the door, lowering her voice. "Small towns. Closed circles. Folks don't trust what they don't know."

I pulled the brim of the cap down.

Outside, the morning air had warmed. Cicadas buzzed in the trees. "It'll take time," she said, lifting my chin so I had to meet her watery blue eyes. "You hear me?"

When I nodded, she hugged me and hurried to her car.

I slid into mine and pressed my forehead against the steering wheel. The vinyl was hot. My head throbbed, and I let the sobs come. Ugly, shaking, unstoppable.

How many times could one child be questioned before he believed he was the problem?

By the time I drove back through town, Home was awake. Sidewalks filled with joggers, strollers, and leashed dogs. Laughter drifted from a coffee shop. People waved to each other—easy smiles, easy belonging for everyone. Except strangers. Especially strangers like us.

I pulled up to our new house, parked in the driveway, and sat still. "I just need a break, God," I whispered.

Chapter 23

I sat at the kitchen nook with my second cup of coffee, school forms spread in uneven stacks before me. The clock above the stove ticked loudly enough to feel personal. Each second carried the same two truths. Owen wasn't home yet, and Lord willing, he would be soon.

The coffee had gone lukewarm. I'd read the same paragraph three times and retained nothing.

Outside the window, wild daisies crowded the side of the old barn-turned-garage, their white heads bright against graying wood. An antique tractor sat half-swallowed by tall grass, its back wheels sunk deep in ruts like it had given up trying to move years ago. A splintered wooden sign dangled from the seat—Maynard—letters bleached nearly invisible by sun and seasons.

A white fence framed the yard. Two magnolia trees stood guard near the meadow beyond, a field that once grew something useful but now lay flat and idle. The nearest neighbor sat a football field away. Close enough to see. Far enough not to hear.

Two chickens scratched in the neighbor's dirt. A rooster strutted and crowed like he owned the morning.

The front door opened.

I didn't turn. I wrapped both hands around my mug and waited.

Owen stepped into the kitchen carrying the scent of bacon and dishwater soap. He dug into his pocket and handed me a crumpled sheet torn from an order pad. "Ms. Dee said to give you this," he said. "In case a situation arises."

I ignored the edge in his voice and unfolded the paper. Her cell. The diner. Her house. Beneath the numbers: TALK TO HIM. All caps. Underlined. On the back: TALK TO YOUR MOM. Underlined twice. I placed it atop the school paperwork. "Can we talk?"

"Right, now?" He leaned against the sink, hands shoved into his pockets, eyes locked on the ticking clock. His long legs stretched across the narrow galley kitchen, nearly touching the cabinets opposite him.

"You can sit," I offered and sipped my lukewarm coffee. "And we can talk."

"I'd rather not. I'm tired."

"Owen, I'm sorry."

He rubbed his eyes. "I'm tired from the day and from everything."

"Look, I was wrong." I stood. The floorboards creaked under my weight. "I admit, I jumped to conclusions."

"You always do."

"That's not fair."

He pushed off the sink and crossed toward the back door, then turned. "You said you believed me. Remember? 'If you're telling the truth, I believe you.'"

The image flashed. Handcuffs, red lights, neighbors watching from within their suburban homes behind their designer curtains.

"Ever since Dad died," he continued, voice tightening, "and I messed up, you don't trust me."

"That's not—"

"Don't." He shook his head. His eyes were rimmed red. "I see it in your eyes. Every time something happens. You look at me like you're waiting for the other shoe to drop." His jaw clenched. "Do you even see anything good in me?"

"Of course I do." I toyed with the half-empty mug, trying to think of what to say next. "It's just that…"

"Never mind." He turned and walked down the hall. "I'll tell Ms. Dee we talked." His bedroom door slammed. The sound traveled through the small house like a gunshot.

I followed and threw open the door without knocking. Owen lay flat on his back on the bed nearest the door. Scotty sat across from him, glasses dangling from one hand, book in the other. He glanced between us. "I'll read somewhere else."

"Scotty," I said softly. "Please shut the door behind you."

Once the door closed, I crossed the room and slapped Owen's socked feet hard enough to startle him upright. "Enough!"

He sat up and stared at me, stunned.

"I'm tired of walking on eggshells," I said, hands braced on my hips. "I messed up. You messed up. We both did. But I cannot pretend the arrest didn't happen. Trust doesn't snap back into place because we want it to."

He drew his knees up, arms wrapping around them like armor.

"Your father's death broke all of us," I said and drew in a breath, noting that the room reeked of cardboard, sweat, and cologne. "But you and your dad—" My voice caught. "You had something special. Sometimes I was jealous of."

"I doubt that." His brow furrowed.

"It's true. You went to him for everything. Bumps, grades, heartbreak. You'd shout, 'I want Daddy,' before I could even get to you. I thought I'd failed you somehow."

"Mom," he muttered.

"Scotty liked me," I said with a weak, watery laugh. "Destiny needed me. But you…" I rolled my shoulders back. "You were his."

The silence thickened.

"When he got sick, you got angry. At the world. At God. At me." I swallowed. "Then one day you weren't a boy anymore. Everyone keeps telling me you're a man, and it's true. You are a man." My voice cracked. "But I don't know when that happened. I don't know when I lost my little boy."

Tears blurred the room. I sat.

He moved to sit beside me. For a moment he just sat there, elbows on his knees. Then he turned and looked at me. Really looked.

"That's the first time you've said that."

"Said what?"

"That I'm a man." He nodded once. "Thank you, Mom."

He grabbed a T-shirt from Scotty's bed and handed it to me. "We're out of tissues."

I pressed it to my face. "Is this clean?"

He shrugged. "I doubt it. It's not mine," he said. "Scotty's."

Despite myself, I laughed through the tears.

He grew serious again. "I screwed up. I know that. But I'm trying, Mom."

"I know," I whispered. "I'm trying too."

He studied me. "I'll tell Ms. Dee we talked."

I got up and walked to the door. "Thanks for hearing me out."

"We're trying," he said, tilting his head the way Michael used to after we'd resolved a fight. "To be okay."

The resemblance stole my breath.

After I left, I stood in the quiet hallway. Outside, the rooster crowed again. And for the first time since the arrest, since the funeral, I sensed the smallest shift.

Not fixed.

Not healed.

But moving.

Chapter 24

Destiny

I miss my rum.

My rum was purpl. Not dark purpl. Lite purpl like lavinder. Mom let me pik it when I was 10. Daddy said it lookd like a princes cloud. Scotty said it lookd like a grape. I lik grapes so I didnt mind.

My bed was by the window. In the mornin the sun cam in soft and yelow and made shapes on my wall. I had glow in the dark stars on the ceilng. Daddy put them up on a ladder and almost fel and Mom screemed and he laffed. He said, "I'm ok, Bug. I can fly."

I dont hav that ceilng now.

In Home the ceilng is plain and white and too big. At niht it feels like its wachin me.

I miss my closet that stikd a little when you tryed to open it. I miss the smel of my rum. It smeld like strawbery shampoo and crayons and the lavander sprey Mom wuld sprits on my pilow.

Here it smels like new paint and wood and sumthing diffrent I cant nam yet.

I miss Colarado.

I miss the mountins. They wer big and blue and alwys there. Even when I was mad or sad or didnt want to go to school, the mountins were still there. Like they wer sayin, "We got you."

Here ther are no mountins. Just feelds and sky that go on and on and make me feel small insted of safe.

I miss the park by our old hous. The one with the ~~squeeky~~ sqeeuky swing. Daddy wood push me high and I wood say, "Higher!" and he wood say, "Your gonna touch the clouds, Bug." I never did but I likd thinkin I mite.

I miss Ms. Boyd.

Ms. Boyd had soft brown hair and wore long sweters even when it wasnt that cold. She had braclets that made tiny jingle sounds when she moved her hands. When I got nervus she wood tap the desk two times and I wood tap it back and that ment I was ok.

She new when I needed more time. She new when I was just thinkin and not being stuborn. She didnt talk to me like I was a baby. She talked to me like I was Destiny.

When other kids stared she wood say, "Is there a question?" and they wood look away fast.

I wonder if she misses me.

I wonder if my desk is empty or if sumone els sits there now.

I miss the way she wood say, "Good mornin, Miss Destiny," like I was importent.

I dont no if my new techer will say my nam like that.

I miss Daddy the most.

I miss his boots by the door. I miss the way he whistled when he did dishes. I miss the scratchy sound of his beard when he kissed my cheek. I miss how he calld me Bug like it was a secrt between us.

At niht in Colarado I wood hear him walk down the hal. I new his steps. Slow. Heavy. Safe.

Here I hear wind in the trees and wind chimes on the porch and sumtimes cars on the road. I dont hear his steps.

I try to remembr his voice so I dont fourget it. I say it in my hed. "Hey, Bug." I say it over and over so it stays.

Sumtimes I think if we didnt move maybe he wuld no where to find us.

That is a dum thought. I no it is. But it sits in my chest anyway.

I miss the last day befor he dieed. I didnt no it was the last day. If I new I wood hav hugd him longer. I wood hav told him about the ladybug I saw on the window. I wood hav said thank you for fixin Lady B's eye.

Now when I hold Lady B I rub the stiched eye with my thumb. Daddy's stiches are a little croked. I lik that. It means he toucht it.

In my old rum I had ladybug stikrs on my miror. Tiny red dots all around the frame. When I looked at myself I was surounded by them.

Here the miror is plain.

I miss the way snow felt in Colarado. Cold and soft and squeeky under boots. I miss white hot choclet after. I miss church where peple new my nam and didnt tilt there heads when they talked to me.

In Home peple look at us like were a story they havent heard yet.

I dont no if I want to tell it.

I miss my mountins. I miss my purpl walls. I miss Ms. Boyd's jingle braclets. I miss Daddy's boots and whistle and voice in the hal.

I miss how things wer.

Mom says this is Home now.

But my hart still feels like its in Colarado. Like it forgot sumthing and wants to go back and get it.

Maybe harts can be in two places at one time.

Maybe ladybugs can fly that far.

I hope so.

Chapter 25

Destiny skipped from her room and met me in the hallway. "Can we go see Pops?"

I dabbed my face with my shirt. "You want to visit your grandfather today?" Would the day ever end?

"Yes, because I made him something." She held up a brown bag with a ribbon tied around the top.

"Princess, can we wait?" I rubbed my temples, remembering the stack of important paperwork in the kitchen. "I've got to finish your school stuff."

Destiny followed me as I walked back to the kitchen, where she stood in front of my workstation, head down, brown bag by her side.

"Come here," I said, and pulled her onto my lap as I examined the school supply lists.

Destiny plopped her bag on top of the lists I'd been reading. "You're not listening to me, Mama."

I stared at her determined face and sighed. Everything in me wanted to find an excuse not to see my father-in-law now or anytime in the near future. But keeping the kids from their grandfather seemed wrong.

"So, today, huh?"

She beamed. "Please, Mama."

Shane McMullen's hardware store had gone days without a visit from me. He encouraged me to get the kids settled and, as far as concern went, that should take a very, very long time.

Scotty, Destiny, and I formed our caravan. Owen remained home, tired and sleeping in his room.

Main Street had settled into a siesta after the morning and noon activities. The outside patio at Dee's sat empty, along with the rockers in front of Pop's. The heat may have aided the emptiness.

The bell jingled as we entered.

"Are you sure this'll work, Shane? I'm so tired of those mice." A man blocked the view of both his purchase and my father-in-law. He stood almost as tall as Scotty, in a blue shirt and faded jeans, filling the space in front of the counter. Work boots completed his outfit, the kind many men in the small community owned.

"Well, now. Haven't had anyone complain yet." Shane's voice came from behind the customer.

Destiny hurried down the aisle, around the counter. "Missed me, Pops?"

"Hold on now. Let me finish up with Zach, here." Shane stepped aside to remove Destiny's arms from around his waist.

She rocked on her heels, held the brown bag, and smiled up at her grandfather.

The customer headed toward the door. Quick glances darted from me to Scotty before he lowered his eyes.

When the bell indicated we were alone, Destiny threw her arms around Shane again for a quick hug.

"I missed you."

Scotty joined them at the counter and extended his hand. "Pops."

Shane paused, studying his grandson. Did he see the boy becoming a man?

"Hi, son." He shook Scotty's hand.

Hugs between them ceased sometime during Michael's illness. Scotty's growth spurt and height difference between them may have contributed to the increased lack of affection that hadn't been much to begin with.

"Where's Owen?" He directed this to Scotty.

"Home. Asleep. He worked at the diner this morning."

Shane's attention shifted to me. "Heard he had a shaky start."

Of course you did. "Just a misunderstanding." I offered a tight-lipped grin.

"Dish boy, huh?"

Silence settled between us.

Destiny held up her present. "For you."

"What's this?"

"Something you need."

"Girl, I really don't need anything." He cast a look my way. "Anymore."

"Call me Destiny. I'm thirteen now. And you do need this." She smiled again.

Shane studied the contents of the bag. "Rocks?"

Destiny shook her head. "Not just rocks." She reached inside and pulled out a stone that easily fit in her palm. "Look at it." One side depicted a face with glasses and curly hair, showing beneath a ball cap. Scotty.

"Dad said you were the rock of your family. Now that we live here, we should be rocks, too."

Shane pulled the rocks from the bag one by one. Owen, Destiny, and then me. He frowned. "There are two more rocks in here."

The next one was Michael's.

"Why are his ears so big?"

Destiny covered a giggle. "Those aren't ears. They're wings."

His focus shifted to the cash register.

"There's one more." My daughter shook the bag toward him.

"Who's this?" He held another rock in his hand.

The image remained unclear from my distance.

"It's you," Destiny said.

"I'm frowning."

"Don't you always? Like this?" She pulled the corners of her mouth down. "There's more." Destiny didn't wait for her grandfather. She reached into the bag and pulled out a small box. On the side, she'd written Family. "See? You do need this. You need family."

She placed the rocks inside the wooden container and gave it to Shane. "We all need family and to be togefer."

Chapter 26

A week later, the kids' paperwork was finished, signed, and initialed, immunizations were copied, and emergency contacts were listed twice. I slid the folders into the passenger seat and drove to Champion School just before noon, when the sun turned the world white.

Orange cones blocked half the parking lot, their color violent against the new black asphalt. A man in a sweat-soaked T-shirt pushed a roller across the pavement, painting crisp white lines that gleamed wet in the light. The tar smell rose thick and chemical, clinging to the back of my throat. Even from inside the SUV, I could see sweat darkening the collar of his shirt. He stopped to drag a red bandana across his forehead, then bent again to his task.

Another hot one. Despite the Fall.

Champion—Home of the Soaring Eagles—was painted in chipped red letters across a brick façade bleached by years of sun. The front doors stood propped open with cinderblocks. Heat poured out in a slow, suffocating breath as I stepped inside.

The air didn't move. It tasted stale, like old textbooks, floor wax, and something faintly sour beneath it. I fanned myself with Destiny's folder and followed a paper sign taped crookedly to the wall: OFFICE →.

The reception area was small enough to take in at a glance. A tall counter with scuffed edges. Three metal chairs that screeched when nudged. A banner on the wall—Welcome to Champion—surrounded by painted handprints in primary colors. Some of the names beneath them had faded to ghosts. On a bulletin board labeled Eagle News, two red sheets of construction paper fluttered weakly beneath the blast of a standing fan. Rectangles of darker red marked where other announcements had once hung.

The fan rotated with a tired groan, pushing around hot air that smelled faintly of mildew.

An inner door stood ajar. I stepped closer.

"Well, I wouldn't have needed to send the staff home if the air worked, Ted."

The voice came from inside. Southern, edged with irritation.

I leaned in. Principal Edwards, his desk plaque announced in brass. He sat tipped back in a high leather chair, socked feet propped on the windowsill, ankles crossed. Two box fans faced him from opposite walls, their roar filling the small office. His tie hung loosened at his collar, shirt damp at the chest.

"The way I see it," he continued into his phone, "every day I send staff home because it's too hot to work is a day off your bill."

I raised my voice. "Hello?"

Nothing.

"Don't think the superintendent will like that? Might hurt your commission."

I rapped my knuckles against the doorframe.

The chair lurched. He grabbed the desk, but the phone slipped from his hand and clattered to the floor. He stared at me, startled, then held up a finger. "One second." He bent, scooped up the phone. "Ted, I'll call you back. Tomorrow's fine."

After ending the call, he removed his glasses and tossed them onto a stack of papers. "Air went out yesterday. Third time this month." He stood, wiping his palm down his khakis before offering it to me. "Jack Edwards."

His handshake was warm, almost slick. The heat had weight in the room, pressing against my shoulders.

"Ebony McMullen. My daughter starts school this semester." I gestured toward the empty reception area. "There wasn't anyone out front."

"Had to send them home." He loosened his tie further, as if it might be strangling him. "No sense in roasting teachers alive."

The corner of his mouth twitched into something like a smile. "I promise we're more welcoming when the air works."

"I brought Destiny's paperwork." I handed him the folder.

He glanced at the name on the tab. "Destiny McMullen. She'll be with Ms. Canter."

"You know her teacher already?"

He shrugged, his expression sheepish. "Easy when there's only one new middle schooler."

I lowered myself into the chair across from him, the metal seat warm from the air. "Only one?"

"We're a small school," he said, his voice gentle. "There are forty-five middle schoolers. About eighty-five elementary students are in the other building. High school across the street—maybe a hundred and twenty on a good year." He studied me for a second, as if gauging my reaction. "Small means we notice when someone's hurting. Or struggling. Or shining."

Through the open window came the distant scrape of the line painter's roller and the metallic clink of his tray. Somewhere down the hall, a locker door banged in the heat.

My gaze drifted to the wall behind him, framed photos of graduating eighth-grade classes. Most rows were barely two deep. Fifteen kids, maybe fewer. The same handful of faces appearing again in elementary photos nearby, just older, taller.

"Our kids," he pointed to photos I'd been staring at. "They won't get lost here," he added.

The thought pressed against something tender inside me.

"I'd introduce you to Ms. Canter, but—" He gestured vaguely at the fans.

"I understand." I stood, my blouse sticking to my back. "I've got to take my son's folder to the high school."

"I can take that." He tapped his watch. "Fall hours. They're about to close up."

"I don't want to trouble you."

"You're not." He stepped past me into the reception area, the fans' roar fading behind us. He placed Destiny's folder on his desk, then tapped a tray labeled HS Mail – Outgoing. A few Manila envelopes lay inside.

"Mrs. Cunningham runs the mail across the street every morning," he said. "I'll make sure this gets there."

I hesitated, then set Owen's folder into the tray. The paper made a soft, final sound as it landed.

"Mrs. Cunningham," I repeated. "She wouldn't happen to be related to Hank Cunningham?"

His eyes lifted to mine. "That's her husband. Y'all met?"

Heat flushed up my neck, hotter than the building. "Yes," I said carefully. "We have."

Something flickered across his face. Curiosity, maybe but he didn't press.

Outside, the cicadas screamed in the trees. The sun hit me like an open oven door, yet somehow the air felt easier to breathe than inside those brick walls.

I glanced back once at the faded eagle painted beside the entrance, wings stretched wide over a school fighting to stay cool, to stay open, to stay alive.

Small towns didn't just remember your name.

They remembered your story.

Chapter 27

Morning came wrapped in a thick fog, thick enough to taste. The cool autumn air and humidity pressed against my skin like a damp quilt as I stood on the porch and watched Owen pedal toward Main Street and his job at the diner.

After one week of training, he'd negotiated his start time from five-thirty to six-thirty. A victory.

The sun hovered just below the horizon, spilling a pale wash of light across the road. No more riding out in total darkness—for now. Fall was already inching toward winter. Soon the mornings would belong to shadows again.

I stepped inside and began the ritual that held my life together. Coffee first, crisis second. The pot gurgled to life. Within minutes, hazelnut filled the narrow galley kitchen, warm and nutty and far more comforting than my current circumstances. I poured a cup and leaned against the sink, breathing it in like oxygen. My favorite mug warmed my hands. I rotated it and read the printed words, "Life begins at the end of your comfort zone."

I glanced at the ceiling. "Are we there yet?" A water stain the size of a dinner plate glared back at me. Someone—fine, me—had tried to paint over it. The brushstrokes formed pale ripples that did nothing to disguise the darker rings beneath. Two more stains decorated the kitchen—one above the table, one by the back door—like a trio of judgmental halos.

I set down my mug, dragged a chair over, and prepared to inspect the damage more closely. That's when I heard it. A faint scratch. A shuffle. I froze.

In the corner beneath the sink, a small brown creature with enormous ears and bead-black eyes sat upright and twitched its pink nose in my direction. I climbed onto the chair so fast I nearly launched it backward. It ran toward me. I screamed. It disappeared under the cabinet. "No, no, no." I scrambled from chair to countertop in one athletic move I will never repeat. Pressed flat against the backsplash, I scanned for movement.

"Mom?"

I jerked upright and smacked my head against the cabinet above me.

Pain exploded across my scalp. Tears sprang to my eyes.

"Rat," I whispered through clenched teeth.

"What?" Scotty stood in the doorway wearing a tank top, baggy shorts, and a backward baseball cap. He looked exactly like he'd fallen asleep mid-basketball game.

"Under. There." I pointed dramatically.

He dropped to all fours and peered beneath the cabinet.

"Be careful," I hissed.

He sat back on his heels. "Good news—he's gone."

I exhaled.

"And there's a hole."

Of course, there was. I eased down from the counter while Scotty gathered packing paper from the pantry. We stuffed the opening as tightly as possible.

"Temporary," I said, pressing the last wad into place.

"Very temporary," he replied.

Destiny wandered in, curls wild, eyes half closed. "Why's everybody yelling?"

"I'm a hero," Scotty said. "Saved Mom from a ferocious beast."

"I found a rodent."

Destiny yawned. "Oh. You met Mickey."

I stared at her. "Excuse me?"

"He lives there." She pointed directly at our paper barricade. "He's not a rat. He's a mouse."

"Princess," I said carefully, kneeling to her level, "why didn't you tell me there was a… mouse… living in our house?"

She shrugged. "He was here first. I thought we could share."

The words that left my mouth next weren't appropriate for morning devotions.

"Mother," Scotty gasped, covering Destiny's ears.

Destiny's eyes widened. "You said bad words."

I pressed my fingertips to my throbbing scalp. "I'm going to your grandfather's hardware store." I held a finger up. "Mickey is not a pet. Do not remove the barricade. Do not name any additional wildlife."

Another storm rolled across the horizon as I drove toward town. Fat drops of rain splattered the windshield three blocks from the store. At the next stop sign, the SUV sputtered. Coughed. Died. I stared at the dark clouds gathering overhead. "God, if you're trying to teach me something," I muttered. "You've made your point." I grabbed my purse and ran.

Two blocks in humidity is a poor life choice. By the time I reached Pops Hardware, rain soaked me to the bone. I burst inside, bent over, hands on knees, breathing as if I'd just completed a marathon.

"Not sure you should be out walking in this weather."

Shane stood behind the counter holding a work towel. He looked as dry and immovable as the shelves around him. "You look like a drowned rat," he added.

I straightened slowly. "Nice to see you too, Shane."

He handed me the towel. "Are your kids okay?"

"Yes. Why wouldn't they be?"

"Too early for a social visit." His green eyes flicked toward the door. "Everything alright at the diner?"

"They're fine," I said, wiping rain from my face and scanning the store, noticing how modern the place was looking. "We have a mouse."

He blinked once. "You've got mice."

"One," I emphasized. "Singular."

He nodded toward the aisle labeled Infestations. "Field mice been bad this year. Especially near the Franklin place. Corn fields will do that."

"They haven't grown corn in years," I muttered, following him.

He picked up two snap traps and held them out. "Set these where you've seen it."

"I promised my daughter I wouldn't kill it."

He stared at me for a long moment. "You can't have it both ways," he said finally.

I hesitated. Destiny's hopeful face floated through my mind. Mickey the Housemate. "Is there a more humane option?" I asked.

He grabbed a small catch-and-release trap from the shelf and added it to the others. "This one keeps it alive. You drive it far enough away, maybe it won't send for reinforcements."

"Reinforcements?" My voice climbed an octave.

"Usually there's more than one."

"No, there's only one," I insisted weakly.

He studied me. The same green eyes Michael had. The same ones Owen carried when he was thinking too hard. "No charge," Shane said quietly when I reached for my wallet.

I looked up. "Thank you."

He nodded once and walked toward the door. The rain had softened to a drizzle. "Are you walking?" he asked.

"I had to. The SUV died two blocks away."

He glanced toward the road, then back at me. "Sounds like you're walking.

Chapter 28

My day ended with new spark plugs, a fuel ignition check, and Mickey the mouse captured by Scotty and relocated far beyond our property line.

The last days of the fall break arrived in a stack of paperwork across my bed. School supply lists. Emergency contact forms. And one bright orange sheet that refused to be thrown away. Volunteers needed.

What I needed was another job.

My art teaching certification was still good, and I could easily supplement my job as a part-time online instructor for a fine arts school in New York. I gathered the papers and walked into the family room.

Scotty sat on the edge of the couch, remote in hand, leaning as if his body could steer his character on the screen. Destiny leaned with him, clutching her ladybug pillow.

"Scotty," I warned.

"Not too violent," he said as his avatar fired. Explosions filled the room. Animated bodies fell.

"Really?"

A sharp tone signaled his digital death.

"No." He slapped the remote against his thigh.

I stepped between them and the television. "We agreed. No violent games when your sister is watching."

Destiny tugged the remote from his hand. "My turn."

"We're switching to another game," Scotty said quickly. "I just wanted one round."

"If she has nightmares, she's sleeping in your bed." I sat in the barrel chair and studied my son. "How would you feel if I worked at your school?"

He scowled. "Like I was being babysat."

"I'm going to start as a volunteer to get my foot in the door. But without your dad's income, my part-time teaching job at the Institute won't cut it for very long." I sighed. "I'm going to apply for teaching jobs at all the schools nearby."

"Nothing I can do about that mom." He reached behind the couch and handed me several wrinkled forms. They were already filled out. "I found out they have a decent football team."

"How did you get these?" I asked as I glanced through the paperwork.

"I printed them."

I scanned the pages, searching for a reason to refuse. There was only one blank line left. Parent signature.

"My physical is still good," he said. "They offer scholarships. I can get help with gear."

He scooted closer. His knee touched mine. "Mom, I'm the new kid. And there aren't many new kids. At least this will help me fit in."

I studied his face. There was no sadness there. There was something steadier. Determination. "What if you get hurt?"

"I'm fast. My football experience gave me that."

I closed my eyes briefly. "I don't know…"

He produced a pen. "Today's the last day to sign up."

I hesitated to take the pen from him.

"Mom, please."

My gaze drifted to Destiny. She was already asleep, her head tipped back, lips parted, ladybug pillow clutched to her chest. "I've never understood how she falls asleep so fast," I whispered and scribbled my signature on the form, then handed it back.

Scotty took the form. "Thanks." He gently removed the remote from Destiny's lap and adjusted her blanket.

"Can we go when Owen gets home?" he asked softly. "He can stay with her."

The front door opened.

Owen walked in with a stained grocery bag. "Leftovers," he whispered, nodding toward the kitchen.

The scent of fried chicken filled the air.

"How was work?" I asked.

"Same." He stroked the peach fuzz on his chin. "Might get to work the grill soon."

"That's good."

He shrugged. "Better than dishes."

I looked at Scotty. "Your brother is trying very hard to convince me to let him play —"

"Football," he said and grinned. "What else is he going to do?" Owen poured a glass of water. "If you say yes, I will buy his cleats." He walked down the hall before I could respond.

Scotty threw his arms up at the television in silent celebration. "I won."

Within minutes, we were in the car, headed to Jefferson High, home of the Knights.

The high school stood across the street from the middle school, both buildings brick and nearly identical, except the high school carried a partial second floor. We found the football office. Ray Reynolds. Geometry teacher. Head coach.

Mr. Reynolds was a barrel-chested man with short red hair and a sparse beard that tried to cover childhood freckles. His arms carried the same red splotches under a heavy tan. A white polo with navy stitching above the pocket identified him as Knights Football Coach.

After quick introductions, Scotty handed him the forms.

Mr. Reynolds rubbed his chin and studied my son. He proceeded to explain the history of the team, expectations, and the consequences of misconduct. We were the only three in the room, but he spoke with enough volume to address a stadium. I checked my watch and tried to cut in. "Mr. Reynolds—"

"Call me Coach Ray." He interlocked his fingers over his abdomen.

"Scotty has always played football," I said.

"Always," he repeated. "Are you fast?"

"Yes," Scotty said.

Coach Ray nodded. "Around here, son, you say yes, sir."

Scotty glanced at me. "Yes, sir."

"Respect is everything." He grinned. "It can take you places and keep you out of trouble." He winked in my direction. "I'm sure this little lady raised you right."

I gripped the strap of my purse. "You won't need to worry about respect, Mr. Reynolds—"

"Coach Ray." He motioned for me to repeat it.

I looked at Scotty. *You've got to be kidding me.* I sighed. "Coach Ray. We just moved here and Scotty doesn't have any equipment."

"Don't worry, little lady—"

"Mrs. McMullen."

Scotty bumped my shoulder.

"We supply most of what he'll need." Coach Ray turned to Scotty. "Got cleats?"

"No, sir. But my brother's buying me some."

I opened my mouth. Scotty stepped slightly in front of me.

"You'll need them by tomorrow. Check the paperwork for practice times." He handed Scotty a small packet. "If you're late, the whole team runs."

Scotty folded the papers under one arm and extended his other hand.

Coach Ray shook it firmly.

"See you tomorrow, sir," Scotty said, steering me out before I could say anything more.

In the hallway, I grabbed his arm. "Are you sure you want to play for that man?"

"Yes."

"You have no idea what you're walking into."

He faced me. The boy in his features battled the young man rising behind his eyes. "You brought us here," he said. "Let me try to find something that's mine."

I exhaled. "I suppose we need new football cleats."

He smiled. "Remember, Owen's buying."

We stepped outside. The practice field stretched beyond the parking lot. A handful of players were already running drills. The sound of helmets colliding carried across the grass.

Scotty stood still, watching.

Coach Ray headed across the field, then turned toward us. He lifted a hand and pointed at Scotty. "We'll see you tomorrow."

Chapter 29

The next morning arrived thick with Carolina humidity and the smell of freshly cut grass.

We pulled into the high school parking lot before the sun had fully burned through the haze. A whistle pierced the air somewhere beyond the brick buildings. The metallic clang of lockers echoed faintly from inside.

Scotty barely waited for the car to stop rolling. He shoved open the door, baseball cap already pulled low, his brand-new cleats slung over his shoulder by their laces. They thumped against his back as he jogged toward the cinder block entrance.

"I love you!" I called.

If he heard me, he didn't show it.

For a moment, I sat there gripping the steering wheel. The vinyl hot against my palms. Sweat gathered at the back of my neck. I could still picture him standing on the practice field the day before, staring at the helmets colliding like thunder.

I shifted into drive.

Across the street sat Champion School. The freshly paved parking lot smelled faintly of tar warming in the sun. Bright white lines cut across the asphalt like boundaries drawn on purpose. I parked and studied Destiny in the rearview mirror.

She stared out the window, clutching her ladybug pillow to her chest.

"Ready to meet your new teacher?" I asked lightly.

Silence.

"Destiny?"

She turned slowly. "Ms. Boyd's not my teacher?"

The question cracked something in me.

I unbuckled and twisted in my seat, resting my hand on her small knee. "Princess, Ms. Boyd is back in Colorado."

Her fingers tightened around Lady B. "I want Ms. Boyd."

"Well," I said, forcing cheer into my voice, "I happen to know your new teacher's name."

Her pillow muffled her words. "You do?"

"Yes." I stepped out, opened her door, and helped her down. "Ms. Canter. And I bet she is very nice."

Destiny sniffed. "Does she like ladybugs?"

"Who doesn't?" I tickled her side.

She giggled, the sound bright and sudden. "Can I show her Lady B?"

"Of course."

I took her free hand and grabbed the heavy bag of school supplies. The plastic handles cut into my fingers as we walked inside.

The office no longer looked forgotten. The old Champion banner still hung across the far wall, but the bulletin board now burst with bright blue paper and neon announcements. Fresh flowers perfumed the air, mixing with the sharp scent of copier toner. Wire baskets lined the counter, neatly labeled by grade.

Behind the desk, a woman flipped through a stack of forms.

"Good morning," I said.

She looked up and smiled. "Well, hello there." She stood, smoothing her slacks. Her ice blue blouse matched her eyes. Auburn hair feathered back from her face in careful layers.

"We're new."

"Yes, I can see that." Her cheeks flushed pink. "What I mean is, I've never seen you before." She extended her hand. "Mrs. Cunningham."

"Ebony McMullen. And this is Destiny."

"Nice to meet y'all."

Destiny pressed against my hip.

A door opened behind the counter. A tall man stepped out holding a screwdriver.

"Mrs. Cunningham, when you get a chance, I cannot get that file drawer open." He stopped when he saw me. "Mrs. McMullen, right?" His smile was easy and practiced.

I nodded.

He walked around the counter and crouched slightly toward Destiny. "You must be Destiny."

She eyed the screwdriver with suspicion.

He followed her gaze and straightened. "Mrs. Cunningham, I surrender." He handed over the tool. "Apparently, I am not qualified to fix office furniture."

They shared a laugh as she disappeared into his office.

He turned back to us. His white shirt was crisp, sleeves secured with cuff links. His tie was a sharp shade of blue that brought out his eyes. Below the hem of his slacks were socks. No shoes. He noticed me looking and wiggled his toes. "I hate shoes."

Destiny giggled.

"Hold on." He vanished into his office and returned seconds later wearing glossy black shoes. "Better?"

"Your office," I said. "I am not here to judge."

"We all do," he replied gently. "Even when we do not mean to." His gaze lingered just long enough to make me look away.

I lifted the supply bag. "We were hoping to meet Ms. Canter. I know the official meet-the-teacher is next week, but we are new. And new places can be hard."

He nodded. "Most teachers wander in by eight thirty. Fall hours." He checked his watch.

Destiny tugged my arm and signed bathroom.

He answered without hesitation. "Down the hall on the right."

I blinked. "You know sign language?"

"I know the important words." He smiled. "Ms. Canter is in room 187. End of the hall, left, through the double doors past the cafeteria."

"Thank you," I said and pulled Destiny as I hurried down the hall.

The hallway smelled faintly of bleach and floor polish. Our footsteps echoed against cinder block walls. After a quick stop, we followed the directions until only one classroom remained beyond the cafeteria.

Destiny drifted to the water fountain, pushing the button and laughing at the splash against her lips.

I stepped into the doorway. A woman stood on a ladder fastening a butterfly border above the whiteboard. The tape made a sticky ripping sound as she pressed it down.

"Hello?"

She turned. Red cat eyeglasses framed sharp eyes. Her lipstick matched the frames. Scissors glinted in one hand. "Oh, honey," she drawled, stepping down. "If you're looking for the kitchen staff, the office is back through those doors."

Destiny moved to my side and took my hand.

The woman clucked her tongue. "I don't think you can bring your kid to the meeting."

Heat crept up my neck. "I'm not…" I inhaled slowly, catching the scent of dust and fresh bulletin board paper. "Let's try this again. My name is Ebony McMullen. Are you Ms. Canter?"

"Yes, I am."

"This is my daughter. She'll be in your class after the fall break."

"I'm so sorry." She touched the small cross resting at her throat. "It's just that I assumed you were the new staff working in the kitchen."

"There've been a lot of assumptions this week," I said evenly.

She climbed down the small ladder and hurried toward us. Gray roots haloed her dark curls. "Again, I'm so sorry for the mix-up. I came early to decorate. I've had several interruptions from the cafeteria staff, and I just thought that's where you were headed." She let out a nervous laugh and turned to Destiny. "So, you're my new student?" she asked.

Destiny pressed into my back and nodded.

"What do you have there?"

"A ladybug." Destiny stepped forward. "Her name is Lady B."

Ms. Canter smiled, revealing a small gap between her front teeth. "I like flying insects too. See?" She gestured toward the butterflies decorating the wall.

I handed the teacher the bag of supplies. "We stopped at the high school first. I picked up what you requested."

She set the bag on a desk and glanced around the unfinished room. Bare walls. Desks slightly crooked. A faint smell of glue. "The official time to meet parents is next week," she said. "I'm not quite ready."

"We're not staying."

A silence settled between us, thin and sharp.

We turned toward the door. "Ms. Canter?" I said.

"Yes, dear."

"Never assume."

Her smile froze.

I walked back down the hall with more force than necessary, Destiny's small hand bouncing in mine.

Principal Edwards stepped from the office as we approached. "Did you find Ms. Canter?"

"I did," I said, my voice flat.

He tilted his head. "Something tells me that didn't go as planned."

"Nothing I haven't dealt with before." I shrugged. "Do you still need volunteers?"

His nodded. "I believe we do."

I'm volunteering." I dug through my purse and pulled out the bright orange form that had haunted my bedroom for days. The paper crinkled in my grip.

"That's mighty generous."

"I'm also a K-12 certified art instructor." I handed him a manila envelope containing my resume, copies of my certification, and several reference letters. "I've been teaching for fifteen years, and I've got an excellent record."

"Good to know," he said as he took the paper. "We don't have any current vacancies. But I'll keep my eye open."

I leaned closer. "One more thing."

"Yes, ma'am?"

"Don't even think about arranging for me to volunteer in the kitchen."

For a moment, he seemed startled. "Of course. I'll make a note of that," he said, laughing.

Chapter 30

I pulled into the practice lot with Scotty beside me, unusually quiet, his workout bag wedged between his knees. I slowed near the curb, expecting him to hop out the way he always did—quick hug, quick "Love you, Mom," and a jog toward the field.

Instead, he unbuckled slowly and glanced past the windshield.

A sleek silver SUV had just parked two spaces ahead.

Before I could ask what he was looking at, Scotty opened his door. But he didn't head toward the field. He veered toward the SUV.

A tall brunette cheerleader stepped out of the passenger side. Long before I could ask what he was looking at, Scotty opened his door. But he didn't head toward the field. He slowed near the passenger side just as the door swung open.

A tall brunette cheerleader stepped out. Long ponytail. Perfect posture. That effortless kind of confidence girls her age rarely have unless they've grown up knowing they're watched.

She said something. Scotty laughed—the easy laugh he saves for people he's already decided he likes.

They walked toward the field together. Not side by side exactly. Just close enough to talk.

I didn't move. My blinker ticked into the quiet of the car. My gaze shifted back to the silver SUV. Custom plates. Immaculate shine. A booster decal on the back window. And then it clicked. Brunette. Cheer squad. Confident.

The coach's daughter.

My grip tightened, my pulse thudding behind my ears.

Oh no.

If that was the coach's daughter, This wasn't just two teenagers talking. This was politics. Locker room dynamics. Playing time. Favoritism whispers. Drama waiting to hatch.

"Is that his girlfriend?" Destiny asked.

I didn't answer.

My stomach flipped.

"Mama, the diner. You promised," Destiny said, pulling me out of my thoughts.

"Okay, Princess." To get Scotty to practice early, I'd bribed Destiny with pancakes at the diner. I sighed and clicked the signal left instead.

***

The bell above the diner door jingled as we stepped inside. Bacon crackled on the griddle. Sweet bread and maple syrup hung thick in the air. Coffee steamed from nearly every table. My body leaned toward it like a plant toward sunlight.

We waited beneath the sign that read "Please wait to be seated."

Katy hurried over in her bubblegum pink uniform and white apron, gum snapping between her teeth. Her brown hair was braided neatly down her back. "Morning. Y'all, we're pretty packed today."

I nodded and followed Destiny's gaze.

She spotted Shane at a booth near the window and took off running. "Pops!"

"Careful, girl, I've got coffee," he muttered, pushing his mug back just in time.

"I'm not girl. I'm Destiny."

I stepped up behind her. "Good morning, Shane."

He nodded once, nothing more.

"Can we eat with you?" Destiny asked, already climbing into the seat beside him. "I can tell you about brother's pretty girlfriend."

"Girlfriend, huh?" Shane arched an eyebrow and kept reading the newspaper spread on

the table before him.

"No, Princess," I said gently. "Katy has a table for us."

Katy hugged the menus to her chest. "Outside seating's all that's left."

Peeking through the glass, metal patio chairs baked in the sun, under the blurry shimmer

of the sun. "We'll eat at the bar."

"Full," she said, popping her gum again.

"We'll wait."

"Could be a while."

Shane huffed and slid his coffee aside. "Just sit."

Before I could protest, Destiny folded her hands primly on the table like she'd been invited to tea. "May I order, please?"

I slid into the seat across from Shane. The vinyl stuck to the back of my legs.

"Pancakes," Destiny said.

"And coffee," I added.

"Is that all you're having?" Shane asked.

"Is that your breakfast?" I countered.

He wrapped both hands around his mug. "Any more mice?"

"No. Scotty relocated him."

Shane tilted his head. "You mean killed?"

Destiny gasped. "Scotty wouldn't kill Mickey."

"You named the rodent?"

Katy arrived with coffee before I had to answer. She set the mug down in front of me. Steam curled upward, creating a temporary veil between Shane and me.

"Food's coming right up." Katy winked at Destiny. "Got a surprise for you, darling."

I closed my eyes and inhaled. The first sip burned in the best possible way.

"Everything okay?" Shane asked.

"It's been a rough morning."

"Is Owen giving you problems?"

"Why must something always be wrong?"

"You're the one who said you had a rough morning."

Before I could respond, Katy returned, balancing a plate high. She lowered it with flair. Chocolate chips spelled Desi across the pancakes. Banana slices formed a wide smile.

Destiny clapped her hands. "Thank you!"

"Not me." Katy jerked her thumb toward the pass-through window.

Dee waved from the kitchen.

"Must be Scotty then," Shane said. "What's he done?"

"Nothing. Why does something have to be wrong?"

"I'm not the one who said rough. Can't I ask about my grandkids?"

"You could start by actually coming to see them," I said and took a sip of my coffee.

His jaw tightened. He reached into his pocket and tossed a couple of bills on the table. "That should cover breakfast for you and your young'un. Good day, Ms. James."

The name hit like a slap. Before I could stop myself, I slammed my hand on the table. Coffee sloshed from my mug. "It's Ebony McMullen," I called after him. "Whether you like it or not, I married your son."

The diner went quiet in that particular way small towns do when something interesting happens.

Shane stopped at the door. He didn't raise his voice. He didn't need to. "No piece of paper will ever make you a McMullen," he said and wedged a toothpick between his lips.

The bell jingled as he walked out.

I sank back into the booth, hands shaking around my cup.

Across from me, Destiny slowly rotated her plate until the banana smile turned upside down. She picked off the chocolate chips one by one and quietly ate them.

After I picked Scotty up from morning practice, I dropped both kids off at home in silence and drove to Lexington. I bought red paint. The brightest, boldest red they had. The kind that demanded attention.

When I'd taken Scotty back for afternoon practice, he'd offhandedly admitted he was dating the coach's daughter when Destiny asked him about it. When I returned to the house, the first coat covered the kitchen walls. The smell of paint filled the house, sharp and heady. I used a sponge, not a brush. Long, determined strokes. Control where I could get it.

Owen walked in just as I finished the last wall.

He stood in the doorway and surveyed the room. "Red, huh."

I shot him a look.

"Just observing," he said quickly, palms up. "Not judging." He stepped closer and ran his fingers lightly over the drying wall. "Want me to clean the brushes?"

"I didn't use any brushes."

"Did you paint the entire kitchen with a sponge?"

I nodded and took a quick stretch break before resuming the kitchen transformation.

"Nice job," Owen said. "It's crazy how paint can transform a place." He cleared his throat. "I'm assuming that breakfast with Pops didn't go too well. I saw you sit with him."

I scrubbed at the red specks around my nails with a paper towel. "Sitting with your grandfather wasn't my idea." I tossed the sponge into the trash.

"Okay, then," Owen said carefully. "New topic. How was the school visit?"

I pressed the lid onto the paint can, struggling with the seal. "I signed up to volunteer. Your brother has a new girlfriend, who I confirmed is the coach's daughter."

"You don't sound thrilled." With one firm smack, he secured the lid for me. "Isn't this what you wanted? For us to fit in and find our way?"

I dropped into a chair and propped my feet on another. "Of course, but I don't understand this place."

He glanced around the kitchen. "You mean the red?"

"No." I gestured toward the window. "This place. Home."

"Home is definitely complicated." Owen grabbed a drink from the fridge. "It seems like everything stays the same, yet everything is changing."

"What do you mean by that?"

"For one, many of the people seem stuck in some strange time warp. It's as if life is passing them by, and they haven't noticed. Owen took a swig of the drink and wiped his mouth. "Then have you noticed how rundown some of these neighborhood stores are. But Grandpa's hardware store is getting all of these renovations?"

I knit my brow, recalling how spiffy Shane's store had been looking lately, but was embarrassed that I hadn't noticed much of what Owen described. "I've noticed a few things. Why?"

"Did you know Pops was into investing in real estate?"

"No, I didn't." I turned to stare at him. "I thought he was trying to wind things down and retire."

"Looks like he's just getting started."

"How?"

"He's added an entire new wing to his apartment at the store." Owen whistled. "It's all top of the line. Granite countertops, high-end fixtures, the works." He took another drink and put the bottle on the counter. "Did you know he bought most of the stores on the same block where his business is?"

"Had no idea," I said, examining the paint caked under my nails. "How'd you find all of this out?

"Through Dee." He threw the empty bottle into the garbage. "I think Pops is pressuring her to sell her diner to him. Sounds like he's got some hook-up with these fancy investors."

"Is she thinking of selling?" I got up and began cleaning my mess.

"If she is, it won't be to him."

I squeezed red paint into the sink and stared at him, trying to conceal my shock. "Why, aren't they friends?"

"Dee's smart. She acts like everyone is her friend, but she's more guarded than she lets on, but she doesn't trust easily."

I rubbed my forehead. "I must say that I'm surprised, but I guess Dee and your grandfather have a right to their own lives."

"What about you, Mom. What do you want here?"

"I just want what's best," I said quietly. "For you. For Scotty. For Destiny."

"But what do you want for yourself?"

I stared at him, trying to figure out what to say.

"You spend all your time taking care of everyone else. Have you ever thought about taking care of yourself and figuring out your purpose here?"

I opened my mouth to answer, but he left the room before I could.

Chapter 31

By way of a lot of encouragement, Owen had accompanied Scotty to the barber. They both returned with new looks.

Scotty's decision to cut his hair so short came hard for me. High and tight, he called it as he rubbed his hand over his head. No curls, no waves, nothing of the styles he'd worn in the past. His scalp showed enough to reveal his birthmark above his ear.

"The helmet will be too hot with long hair."

His curls will grow back. The words became a mantra.

Owen had his sides cut short but left the top long and pulled back in a man bun. Natural highlights streaked the top of his taut hair. The straight parts on both sides of his head exposed his tanned skin and the skills of an expert barber.

"I can wear a cook's cap instead of a net now." His reason for the new style.

"The local barber, Coach Reynolds, recommended cutting your hair like that?"

Laundry kept my hands busy. An older gentleman with stark white hair, clean-shaven, was my image of a barber in Home. He could do Scotty's cut, but Owen's? No.

"Not exactly." Owen glanced at his brother.

I dropped a towel in the basket a little harder than I'd meant. "What does that mean?"

"I met a couple of local guys at the diner. They told me about another barber," Owen said.

"Another barber?"

Scotty wouldn't look in my direction.

Owen shoved his hand in a pocket. "You know."

"If I knew I wouldn't be asking."

"The locals were Black. They mentioned a shop at a guy's house."

I held the next towel in midair. "You took your brother to a stranger's house to get a haircut?"

"Mom, you said I could get a cut."

"You said you were going to the barber Coach Ray mentioned."

"He planned to." Owen sat on the couch and placed a paper bag next to him. "I told him about FAM, and he was willing to go."

"FAM?"

"Short for Fade Masters, that's what the locals call it." Scotty offered.

"Uh-huh. And where exactly did the locals send you?"

"I'll help." Scotty grabbed the stack of linen, headed down the hall, and left me with his older brother.

"Well." Owen cleared his throat. "Welcome."

I moved the basket of unfolded clothes. "Exactly where in Welcome?"

"A barbershop. Like I said."

"No, you said a house. You decided to head out of town without telling me? Your phone no longer works?"

"It's only fifteen minutes away. If I called, then what? You would have said?"

"No."

"That's why I didn't."

I leaned toward him. "And you wonder why I don't trust you."

Owen narrowed his eyes and stood. "Nice one, Mom. By the way, Mr. Wilson said to tell you hello. He was at FAM. His son owns the place."

My mouth opened.

Owen shook his head. "Don't bother." He left the room.

The paper bag remained on the couch. I grabbed the bag to give to Owen and apologized for the umpteenth time. A familiar scent stopped me. A look inside revealed Loretta's fried pies.

Scotty returned. Leaned on the wall by the hallway. "Owen thought you and Destiny might like some. We stopped by the store. He's been helping the Wilsons out. Mr. Rob even hinted that he'd love for Owen to manage the store. Maybe even buy it one day. He shrugged. "Who knows." The words came flat, his gaze hardening into something accusing.

My misjudgment prevented me from eating one.

"Is Owen in your room?"

"I came to tell you he's packing."

"What!" Using the wall to steady myself, I headed to my sons' bedroom.

An open duffel sat at the end of Owen's bed. Pieces of clothing stuck out. He reached into a drawer, lifted out shorts, and tossed them toward the bag.

"Owen. Please."

"No."

One word and a hostile look kept the distance between us.

"Where will you go?" The question came out rough and strained.

He yanked a jacket from a hanger with so much force that the wire holder bounced out of the closet and stopped inches from my feet.

My attempt to bend the twisted form back into the original shape became a lost cause.

"Why bother staying?" He clenched a pair of jeans in a tight fist. "You don't trust me."

"Why do you bait me? You knew you were going to Welcome. You knew who owned the shop, but you want me to fail."

A hanger flew onto his bed. "No. I want you to trust me."

"How can I when you won't let me?"

"You can't let go of the past," he shouted. Owen crammed the jeans in the duffel and attempted to close the bag.

Tears threatened to spill. "You won't let me." I fired back.

"O?" Destiny stood by the door with Lady B held to her chest. "Why are you packing?" Her gaze shifted between us. "Why are you yelling?" She moved closer to her brother. "Did you make Mama cry?"

He crouched down to her level.

Destiny toyed with the band that held her brother's hair in place. "I like your haircut. Are you leaving?"

"Desi, sometimes family members need to move out."

"Why?" She pulled the band off Owen's hair. More waves than curls fell near his face.

"They just do." He tucked the loose strands.

Destiny shook her head. "But it's not time."

My son and I exchanged looks.

"What do you mean?"

"Did you plan on leaving today?" She leaned her head on his shoulder.

"No." He gazed at the duffel.

"Then the time is wrong."

He pulled Destiny from his shoulder. "Sometimes things happen."

"Did Mama ask you to leave?"

"No. She asked me to stay."

"Okay. Hold, please." Destiny handed me her pillow, then sat next to Owen's bag.

"I'll help you unpack."

"Please," I mouthed.

"I will be moving out. Soon." He stood.

"Not today." She picked up the destroyed hanger. "Do you want to use this one?"

Chapter 32

Pizza for dinner had left me with nightmares and heartburn. Dreams of Owen leaving, but somewhere in the craziness of my dream, Michael would be the one who walked out the door. Jerking awake for the third time came with a moan and a grab for the phone to check the time. Too early to get up, but too late to fall back asleep.

Our neighborhood's rooster crowed. That animal was earning my disdain.

I pulled the pillow over my head. Breathing steadied. Relaxation came. But soon the mattress moved, and one side of the pillow lifted.

Destiny rested her cheek on my bed.

"What's wrong, Princess?" Sitting up allowed both of us to get comfortable.

She climbed onto the bed and snuggled.

"You, okay? Where's Lady B?"

"With O."

"Why?"

"He needed the company."

"He did?" I chuckled.

"Huh-uh. Thought he would get lonely in the barn."

The words almost sent Destiny tumbling off the bed. "He slept there?" Princess, is he still out there?"

"Think so." Her small fists rubbed drowsy eyes, followed by a yawn.

I tucked her in and slipped out the back door.

Our barn contained space for our SUV on one side and evidence where stalls had been on the other, along with a few stored items, a polite way to say junk. To slide the large door would tell Owen someone was checking on him. Or even worse, wake him. I hiked up my pajama pants and stepped through the wet grass to peer in the window. The once clear panes, now covered in mold and dirt, made visibility impossible.

A path led to the back of the structure, past Maynard the tractor, to the rear door. Locked. No way of knowing whether Owen or the SUV were where they were supposed to be. The coolness of the morning had given me a chill, and protecting my PJ bottoms was in vain. A ring of moisture, along with pieces of grass, hugged the lower part of each leg.

The field in front produced a yellow glow as the sun rose from the front of the barn. Birds chirped while a dog barked somewhere far off. My neighbor's rooster crowed again.

A cool breeze blew, rustling the grass against my bare feet. The wind stopped. The sensation over my toes did not.

"Snake!" My scream came repeatedly. Jumping from one foot to the other, with arms waving in a fashion that should never be repeated or witnessed, I launched to the front of the tractor. A long black tail slithered around the corner.

My heart pounded. I drew in a shaky breath.

"Mom?"

Another scream and loss of balance landed me sitting on the ground. Pain shot through my tailbone, while the morning dew now soaked my PJs. The struggle to my feet took effort.

"I stepped on a snake."

"A little early to be out. They're usually around more in the summer." Owen's hair hung loose. Bare-chested, he wore gym shorts that sat low on his narrow hips and exposed the band of his underwear. "Is there another problem?" My son stood inside the open door with arms crossed.

I stood, wiped dirty hands on my pajama pants, and stared in the direction the creature slithered. "I really hate snakes."

Owen, barefoot like me, moved toward the far side of the barn and scanned the shadows. "Probably just a black snake." His gaze shifted my way. "Are you checking up on me?"

Crossing the threshold, damp grass gave way to drier dirt underfoot. At the SUV, I rested my hand on the hood. Cool.

Owen came in behind me. "I don't have the keys."

To the right of the truck, a mattress, covered by a sleeping bag, sat on a sheet of plywood with Owen's duffel in a wheelbarrow nearby. Old farm tools hung on the wall next to his bedding, permanent fixtures and remnants of Michael's childhood.

"When did you bring your mattress out?"

"Late last night." He walked to the duffel, pulled out a red tee, and, in two quick movements, dressed and pulled his hair back.

"Are you going to live out here?"

Something scurried on the ground behind me, and I flinched. I pushed away thoughts of Mickey from my mind. "You don't have to do this."

He slipped on flip-flops, then leaned against the SUV next to me. "The room's too small for both of us, Mom. Scotty needs his own space. We both do. I've thought about staying out here before. Honestly, since we moved."

"Owen, a garage?"

"It's a barn." He spun around as if showing off a mansion. "See, there's plenty of room."

"Why?" A damp, earthy odor hung in the air.

"I needed to."

Something in his expression told me not to push further. "What about the weather and," I searched the ground, "snakes? There's not much insulation out here."

"Mom." He tilted his head and looked at me sideways. "I can take care of myself."

"Scotty's okay with this?"

He scoffed. "Who do you think helped me move the mattress?"

Did my oldest really want to live with cobwebs, spiders, and other outside creatures?

On the other side of the open door stood our neighbor's rooster. The bird cocked his head and crowed. I narrowed my eyes at the intruder. "No roommates, especially critters."

Owen tapped the hood of the car. "This is a bachelor pad."

With the SUV backed into the driveway, Owen spent most of Saturday fixing up his new room. Scotty and Destiny helped.

The rule was simple. No visits until he finished. That meant me. The kitchen nook offered the perfect spot to absorb the sounds of construction while sketching ideas for our red kitchen. Every so often, Destiny slipped inside. "Go to your room."

I raised a brow. "Why?"

"You can't see the decorations." She escorted me to my bedroom, and when the mystery items were retrieved, she'd yell from the kitchen, "You can come out!" At which time, the nook welcomed me back.

Late afternoon, Scotty ran from the garage laughing. Owen chased him with the garden hose—water aimed at his brother. The water stopped as Owen closed in. Destiny stood by the side wall, hidden from the boys but visible to me, her grip tight around the hose. She released it the instant Owen turned the spray toward himself. I laughed, then scrambled for towels. Destiny met me at the door.

"Thanks, Mama. Stay here, please." She scurried off.

I leaned back in the chair with a sigh. The kids were doing what I'd hoped for since Michael died, connecting, enjoying each other. Then the realization that it didn't include me. The sketch pad pushed aside, I replaced it with my Sudoku book.

The same puzzle remained unfinished until Destiny reappeared at the door. She extended her hand. "Come see O's room."

Her brothers stood in front of the sliding door, somber looks on their faces. They glanced at each other, nodded, and pushed open the entrance.

The side of the barn that had held a mattress and a duffel earlier now had a bedroom. A real bedroom. Owen's old basketball jerseys decorated the walls, hung with the help of farming tools. Old milk crates, used for storage, held knick-knacks and folded clothes. Rope lights hung near the rafters. Rugs from our basement covered the floor; the entire space was raised above the barn floor foundation with plywood.

"Wow." I drew out the word.

"We built a platform." Scotty beamed. "I knew you'd worry about everything getting ruined. So, when I found plywood under some tarps, I was able to put it to good use. Hope they weren't needed for anything," Owen said.

"I doubt it. That stuff has been in here for years." I stepped forward.

Scotty held up his hand. "Wait, watch this."

He helped his brother slide two more upright sheets of plywood to create a barrier between Owen's space and the rest of the barn. The sides facing out were decorated with Destiny's artwork.

My daughter clapped. "It's a keep-out wall."

"Privacy wall, Desi," Owen said.

"Nice work." I looked around in awe. With the extra wood secured, my son's own space was complete.

"Doesn't make a full enclosure, but with what was left, I thought it worked," Owen said.

The boys pushed the makeshift doors back against the rear wall.

Their combined effort was impressive. On the crate beside his bed sat the family picture from our end table.

Owen stood beside me. "Destiny brought that out. If you want it back—"

"No. It looks good here. Everything looks good here."

Pride lit his expression.

Scotty punched his brother in the arm. "So, who's going to help me fix up my room?"

"Me!" Destiny said.

Owen dropped onto his bed and locked his hands behind his neck. "Not me, I'm too tired. Now, if you don't mind, I'm going to need some privacy in my place."

His place. I never thought the first one would be a barn.

Chapter 33

Destiny was true to her promise. She helped Scotty rearrange his room to accommodate the extra space he now had, and Owen did eventually join in. They let me help as well. Family bonding at its best.

The youngest member of our family wanted to change her room. We moved her bed from one side to the other. That's all she wanted done.

As we all prepared for bed, exhausted from the day, Owen stepped outside.

"Are you going to be okay, son?"

He rested his hand on the porch railing. "Are you going to ask me that every night?" A grin spread across his face.

"No." I glanced toward the barn. We'd agreed to leave the light on above the door.

"Thanks for letting me have my own space, Mom."

The sound of frogs croaking eased the silence between us as Owen stepped from the shadows of the house into the light of the barn.

I pressed my hand against the tightness in my chest.

He disappeared into his new residence.

The walk toward the bedroom came with a new appreciation for Owen and a heaviness in my heart. Soon, he would choose a new path.

I walked past Scotty's room first. The door was closed, but light spilled out from underneath. *Had he finished Braveheart?* I rested my hand on the door now housed by only one son but didn't knock. Instead,

I continued down the hall toward Destiny's room. Her nightlight danced stars on the ceiling. The pink-and-green patchwork quilt lay half on the floor and half on my child. She rested on her stomach, one leg hanging off the bed. A small desk beside her was covered with markers, papers, and other items from a craft box.

I adjusted her onto the bed before placing a kiss on her forehead. She rolled over and wrapped her arms around Lady B. The walk to my room confirmed we'd all sleep in.

Or not.

Earlier than hoped, a familiar tap on my arm told me one thing. Without opening my eyes, I moaned and rolled away. "Destiny, today's Sunday."

"I know."

How can anyone sound so chipper at—I checked the phone— okay, later than I thought, but still early. Rolled to face her and peeked through half-opened lids.

"Are you hungry?"

She stood next to my bed, dressed in a short-sleeved blouse and her favorite pink skirt. Her attempt at a ponytail left most of the right side of her curls loose and hanging past her shoulder.

"It's Sunday, Mama."

I pushed up against protesting muscles and sat against my headboard. "I know. I just told you that."

"Are we going to church?"

"What?" I asked, stifling a yawn.

"Today's Sunday."

I stretched my arms over my head, "Okay, Destiny, we've established that."

"We've been invited." She handed me a flyer.

"Welcome to Home. We here at Friendly Church would welcome your presence. Please join us." The rest of the information contained an address and a cartoon picture of people entering a building. I knew the place well, Shane McMullen's church.

"Where'd you get this?"

"From the mailbox yesterday."

"Hold on."

The trip to the bathroom provided me time to wake up and figure out how to respond. By the time of my return, Destiny stood by the bed with a coffee mug extended forward. Thank goodness all the children knew how to work the coffee maker.

"Thank you, Princess."

The first sip revealed lukewarm liquid, more cream than coffee. Maybe a lesson in preparation was needed. Back to the flyer.

"We've had a busy week. Still getting settled and working on Owen's room, maybe we should let the guys rest."

"They promised."

Owen walked past the open door, then stepped back. A towel rested around his neck. "Don't you need to get ready?"

I gave Destiny an open-mouthed stare.

She giggled.

I dressed, re-combed Destiny's hair, and still had time for a fresh cup of coffee. Everyone was in the car with plenty of time to arrive at church by eleven.

Chapter 34

When we walked into First Baptist of Home, every head turned.

Not in the curious way. Not in the warm, we're-glad-you're-here way. It was slower than that. Heavier.

We filled an entire row. I sat on the end, Destiny next to me in her ladybug dress, Scotty straight-backed and alert, Owen already distant, like he was somewhere else entirely. The sanctuary smelled of lemon polish and old hymnals. The stained-glass windows cast careful colors across white faces.

Michael used to say small towns were easier. "People see you," he'd tell me.

They saw us.

They just didn't quite know what to do with what they saw.

After the service, hands were shaken. Names exchanged. Smiles offered with lips but not always with eyes. A woman with a tight bun and pearls told me she was "sure the Lord had a reason" for bringing us here. I wanted to ask her if that same Lord had a reason for taking my husband a month ago.

Instead, I nodded.

Destiny tugged at my sleeve. "Momma, she didn't say I look pretty."

"You look beautiful," I whispered.

Across the aisle, I caught sight of Shane.

My father-in-law stood near the double doors, shoulders squared, as if he owned the building. Which, in a way, he did—his donations had built half of it. The brass plaque in the vestibule proved that.

He didn't come to sit with us.

He didn't come to hug his granddaughter.

He gave me a nod. Polite. Distant. The kind you give a tenant.

Shane McMullen was a respected man in Home, North Carolina. Land. Hardware store. Influence. The kind of man who shook hands, and people said yes before he finished speaking.

He was also Michael's father. Since Michael died, something in him had hardened toward us—toward me in particular. As if grief needed somewhere to land, and I was the closest target.

"You settling in?" he asked after church, his tone carrying the weight of obligation.

"We're getting there," I said.

His eyes flicked over the children. Assessed. Calculated. "You'll find people here take care of their own," he said.

I wasn't sure if that was a promise.

Or a warning.

***

Home was small enough that nothing stayed private for long. By the second week, everyone knew Michael had died suddenly. They knew we had come from Colorado. They knew Destiny had Down syndrome. They knew Owen lived in a barn.

What they didn't know was how thin everything felt inside our house.

Or how often I lie awake listening to the empty space on my bed where my husband used to breathe.

The fight that pushed Owen to the barn still echoed in my chest.

It started with dishes. It ended with words that cut.

"You don't get to act like you're the only one who lost him," Owen had snapped at Scotty.

"And you don't get to disappear," Scotty shot back.

Then Owen turned on me. "You can't fix this, Mom."

I tried to hold steady. "I'm not trying to fix it. I'm trying to keep us together."

He laughed, sharp and broken. "You moved us across the country."

"We had no choice."

"There's always a choice."

That was when he said he'd move into the barn.

I thought he was bluffing.

He wasn't.

Now, at night, I see the single light glowing out there across the McCullen property—our property, though sometimes it doesn't feel like it. The barn stands a little way behind the house, red paint faded, tin roof humming when it rains. Owen cleared a space upstairs. Dragged in a mattress. Strung extension cords.

The church ladies brought casseroles the first week. After that, they brought advice.

"You'll want to be careful letting that boy isolate himself," one said.

"Asking questions about the Lord is natural," another offered when I mentioned Owen seemed distant. "But doubt spreads."

Doubt spreads.

Like we were contagious.

The youth pastor asked Scotty if he'd like to give his testimony one Wednesday night— "It would be powerful, son, what you've been through."

Scotty smiled politely. Later, in the truck, he stared straight ahead. "I'm not a project," he muttered.

"No, you're not," I said.

At school, Destiny came home quieter than usual.

"They said my hair is wild," she told me one afternoon, running her fingers through her curls. "I like it wild."

"I like it wild too."

But I saw the way she clung to me in the grocery store, how her bright joy dimmed just slightly in public spaces.

Not everyone was unkind. Dee at the diner had been warm from the start. She hugged Destiny like she'd known her forever. She called Scotty "Quarterback" before he even earned the title. She let Owen fix the air conditioner when it broke and paid him in cash and pie.

Still, there was a line in this town. Invisible. Firm.

And we were on the wrong side of it.

Chapter 35

Shane's hardware store sits square on Main Street, across from Dee's Diner. It's the kind of place where men lean on counters and discuss crops, football, and zoning laws in the same breath.

I started noticing the pattern when I went in to buy a rake.

Shane was in the back office with two men in pressed shirts—city men. Not farmers. Not locals.

They spoke in low voices.

"…before the county catches on."

"…properties near the river are undervalued."

"…once the bypass goes through—"

The door closed when they saw me. Later that week, a For Sale sign appeared on old Mrs. Halpern's place. Two weeks after that, a construction truck from Raleigh was parked outside.

Renovation.

Rumor said investors were sniffing around Home. That land was cheap. That it wouldn't be for long.

One evening at the diner, I asked Shane about it.

"Town's growing," he said evenly. "That's a good thing."

"For who?"

"For everyone."

But his eyes slid away.

Michael used to argue with him about development. Said it would price families out. Said Home would stop being home.

Shane had called him naïve.

Now Michael was gone.

And I was the one sitting at the table.

Shane's father—Michael's father—kept his distance. He'd come by once after we arrived. He walked the entire property, writing down notes in a small black book he shoved in his jacket when I came outside to greet him.

Afterwards, he shook the boy's hands. Allowed Destiny to kiss his cheek. Avoided my eyes.

"I've been busy," he said when I asked if he'd like to stay for coffee.

Busy.

In a town this small, busy usually meant avoiding something.

Or someone.

At church, he sat alone. Not with us.

There were fractures here older than my grief.

And I had walked straight into the middle of them.

Chapter 36

One Saturday evening after cooking a baked chicken for dinner, I walked out to the barn.

The sun bled orange over the fields. Crickets tuned up. The air held a slight chill weighted by dense humidity.

Owen was sitting beside the barn on the tailgate of his newly purchased pick-up truck.

"Are you planning on eating with us?" I asked. "I made your favorites."

His face brightened. "You made baked chicken, mashed potatoes, and green beans?"

I nodded.

"You haven't made that meal since—"

"Dad died. I know."

Owen jumped down from the truck. "I made a batch of oatmeal cookies at the diner. Dees lets me cook sometimes when I'm not fixing something. I'll go grab them out of the truck and bring them for dessert," he said, and hurried to the passenger side to retrieve a pink bakery box.

Once he returned, he opened the box and proudly extended a cookie in my direction. "I'll let you take a taste test before we share them with the others."

I took the cookie and bit into it. "This is delicious," I said, savoring every crumb. "When did you learn to bake?"

"Between Mrs. Loretta and Dee, I've picked up a few things."

"Do you get to see the Wilsons much?" I asked through a mouthful of cookie.

"Yeah, I've been helping fix their place up quite a bit." He frowned. "I think the store is getting to be a lot for them."

"How's Mrs. Loretta?"

"Still sweet. Just slower. She asks about you all the time. But she asks about Destiny more."

"Really?"

"Did you know Destiny sees things?"

I stopped chewing and cleared my throat. "Like what?"

"Like Dad."

I shuddered, remembering Destiny telling me that her father had spoken to her. I'd chalked it up to her imagination. "Did she tell you that?"

"She has. But she's seen other things or people...I'm not sure." He rolled his shoulders back. "She mostly sees things inside the barn."

"Does that scare you?"

He shook his head. "The weird thing is, I think she's right. I do sense a presence here, sometimes more than one. But it's not a frightening experience. I get the feeling that there's something about this place that's layered. Like the barn holds secrets it wants us to know about." He tilted his head. "Do you think I sound crazy?"

"No, honestly, I've always felt that way about this entire place. Especially the barn."

He exhaled. "I'm relieved I'm not the only one. Besides, Scotty mentioned it, too."

I dusted cookie crumbs from my shirt. "Has Desi said anything that stands out to you in particular?"

"She's talked about seeing a woman around the barn."

I shivered and glanced over my shoulder. "That's strange."

"The funny thing is," Owen said, lowering his voice, "Desi told me you have one of the lady's pearls. And that it has a secret inside."

"Very…odd," I said, slowly recalling the pearl Mrs. Loretta had gifted me months ago on our way Home. "I didn't even think she knew what a pearl necklace was. It's not like I own one."

Owen leaned back against his truck, watching the barn the way people watch a storm roll in. "She's been talking about that woman for months. Says she's pretty. Wears a pearl necklace. Sometimes she stands by the barn door."

A chill crawled down my spine.

"The first time Desi said it," he continued, "I thought it was imagination. But then Mrs. Loretta started asking questions."

"What kind of questions?"

"About Destiny. What she sees. When she sees it."

"And?"

Owen hesitated. "She told me something one afternoon when I was helping her stack canned goods in the store. Said I was old enough to know a few things about this town."

The wind moved through the trees, the same slow rustle I'd heard on visits to the property, but this time it seemed louder.

"Mrs. Loretta said her grandmother was born into slavery," Owen said quietly. "Just a baby when the war ended. Her family was freed before she could even remember being owned. But there's this special pearl necklace that was handed down through the family, somehow connecting them to one another."

My breath caught. "How so?"

"She said folks around here like to pretend all that history stayed buried. But it didn't." He nodded toward the barn. "Some of it's right over there. She said that sometimes pieces of jewelry were ways for slave masters to gift the women they had babies with. It was a way for the women to buy their freedom. Other times, it was a way to hide secrets and protect important documents."

"But how can anything like that be connected to the barn?"

He nodded. "Back in the fifties and sixties," Owen said, "Mrs. Loretta and Alice McMullen—Pop's wife—ran a Bible study out there. She said it was more than a study, it was a way to preserve history."

I blinked. "In the barn?"

"Not exactly advertised." Owen gave a thin smile. "Black folks. White folks. All meeting together when some people in town wouldn't have liked it very much."

My eyes drifted toward the wide barn doors, dark against the fading light.

"They kept it quiet," Owen said. "But Loretta told me that the barn had always been a place where people told the truth when the town didn't want to hear it. It used to be a place of hope and unity."

I wrapped my arms around myself.

"Before I left the store that day," he continued, "Mrs. Loretta said something else."

"What?" I asked, leaning forward.

He rubbed the back of his neck.

"She said that Pops has a secret he doesn't want anyone knowing."

My stomach tightened. "What kind of secret?"

Owen glanced at the house, then back at the barn. "She said his great-grandmother was Black."

The words hung in the air like thunder.

I stared at him. "That can't be right."

"That's what I said."

"And?"

Owen nodded slowly toward the barn again. "So, I went digging myself because I didn't want to say anything to you until I could prove it."

My pulse picked up.

"There's a loft up there," he said. "Old trunks. Boxes. Papers nobody's looked at in decades."

"What did you find?"

"Ledgers. Property records. Letters." His voice dropped. "Names that connect Loretta's family to Shane's line."

I felt the ground shift beneath me. "And Dee?" I asked. "Earlier, you mentioned that she might know something."

Owen gave a small, humorless laugh. "I mentioned it to her once. Just testing the waters." He shook his head. "She didn't confirm it. But she didn't deny it either."

The barn creaked in the wind.

Behind us, Destiny's laughter floated from the house.

Owen followed the sound, then looked back at me. "Loretta said some secrets wait a long time to come out," he said. "Sometimes they wait for the right people."

A shiver moved through me as my gaze settled on the barn doors.

Somewhere deep inside the structure, something thudded softly. Wood shifting. Or something else.

And for the first time since coming back to Home, I wondered if the barn wasn't just holding history.

Maybe it was holding the truth.

And maybe Destiny wasn't the only one who could see it.

Chapter 37

The first home game packed the bleachers.

We sat together—me and Destiny, her hands sticky with cotton candy. Owen stood near the fence with friends from the diner. Shane occupied the fifty-yard line like royalty.

When Scotty ran onto the field, the crowd roared.

For a moment, grief loosened its grip.

For a moment, we were just another family under Friday night lights.

But when halftime came, and I overheard a woman say, "They're fitting in better than I expected," the knot returned.

Fitting in.

As if we were shoes.

As if this town were deciding whether we were worth keeping.

Later that night, Shane stopped by the house. He stood on the porch, hat in hand. "Town council's voting next month," he said. "On zoning changes."

"For the river properties?"

His eyes narrowed slightly.

"You've been listening."

"I've been living here."

He exhaled.

"Growth is coming whether we like it or not."

"At what cost?"

He studied me—really studied me—for the first time since the funeral. "You always did ask hard questions," he said.

"I learned from your son."

Something flickered across his face. Grief. Regret. Maybe both. Then it was gone.

"Just make sure y'all have a plan. Make sure your boys are ready for life," he said quietly. "Things are shifting."

He walked back into the night before I could ask what that meant.

Inside, Destiny was asleep on the couch, ladybugs bright against soft fabric.

Owen's barn light glowed steadily. Scotty's cleats sat by the door, grass-stained and hopeful. Home, North Carolina, was changing. So were we.

The church might never fully open its arms. Shane might never close the distance. Shane might be building something bigger than hardware stores and handshakes.

But my children were finding their footing.

Even in unfamiliar soil.

And maybe that was what Michael meant all along.

Not that small towns were easier.

But those roots don't ask permission.

They grow where they're planted, whether this town liked it or not.

Chapter 38

That night, the house felt too quiet. The boys were in their rooms. Scotty down the hall. Owen in the barn. Destiny hummed softly to Lady B in the hallway, the same song she'd sung since Colorado. The tune drifted through the cracked door like a fragile thread trying to stitch the house together.

I sat at the kitchen table with Michael's note in front of me.

The page was worn where I'd traced the words too many times.

Don't trust my brother.

Don't trust Dad.

At first, I'd blamed grief. Stress. A man unraveling under the weight of life. But now the words sat differently. Like a warning.

I tucked the note back into Michael's journal and looked out the window toward the barn.

The moon hung low behind it, silvering the roofline.

Just then, my phone buzzed.

"Hey, Owen, is everything okay?"

"Mom, I think you need to come over and see this."

"I'll be right over," I said, and grabbed my jacket.

The barn smelled like cedar, oil, and something older—dust and history settling into wood.

A lantern flickered beside Owen, who sat cross-legged on the floor with a stack of papers spread around him.

"Good, you came," he said. "I was worried you'd be asleep by now."

"You sounded serious."

"I am." He handed me a ledger.

The pages were yellowed, but the handwriting was sharp. Property numbers. Acreage. Names I recognized. Families in Home and in neighboring towns. The Wilsons. Dee's diner lot. Our house.

"What is this?" I whispered.

"Sales records," Owen said. "Or what will be the sales records."

"How did you get this?"

"Promise you won't judge me first."

"I promise," I said and stared at his face, etched with worry.

"You know how I've been hired to fix things in town?"

I nodded, my hand frozen on the page I'd been looking at.

"I had to pick up a bunch of supplies at Pops' store. He had an important meeting to get to and was rushing me out so he could lock up. He didn't realize he'd left this ledger on the back of his truck and sped off. I grabbed it off the ground and tried flagging him down, but he didn't see me." Owen sighed. "When I started going through the ledger, I realized this was something big."

"It's more than big." I flipped another page. Next to each property was a second column. Numbers. Low numbers. Too low. "And these prices are wrong."

"They're not real prices," Owen said. "They're what Shane's offering people."

"For what?"

"Development. Big developers," Owen said. "Luxury lake homes. Resort property. Golf courses." He tapped the ledger. "Everything around here is worth ten times what he's offering."

My hands started to shake. "He's buying it cheap."

Owen nodded. "And flipping it through Uncle Gabe's company."

The words felt like ice water down my spine. "No."

Owen didn't look away. "Yes."

The barn creaked in the wind.

"He's been doing it quietly for a while," Owen said, his voice low, like he was trying to protect me. "Buying land from people who trust him. Or people who feel pressured."

I thought of Rob and Loretta Wilson. Their tired eyes in the store. Of Dee's tight smile when developers came into the diner.

"Loretta told me something else," Owen continued.

"What?"

"Pops has investors waiting."

"How do you know Gabe's involved?"

Owen hesitated. "Because I saw the transfer."

"What transfer?"

He slid another paper toward me.

My breath left my lungs. The account name was familiar. Michael's life insurance policy. A withdrawal. A large one. Authorized by Gabe. I stared at the number. "That's impossible," I whispered.

"He told the bank he was helping invest it," Owen said quietly. "Said it would grow the money for the family."

Michael's note flashed through my mind. *Don't trust my brother.*

"He used Michael's death." My voice came out thin.

Owen's silence was answer enough.

Outside, the wind rushed through the trees.

I suddenly felt like the barn had closed in around me. "Why would they do this to us?" I whispered.

Owen leaned back against a beam. "Because the developers are offering millions once they have the land."

"And Shane—"

"Gets the properties cheap."

"And Gabe?"

Owen shrugged. "I think Uncle Gabe might have thought it was a legitimate investment."

"Thought?"

"I don't think he understands the full scheme."

My heart pounded. *Michael had known. Somehow, he'd known.*

Chapter 39

The next morning, I drove to the Wilsons' store.

Mrs. Loretta met me on the porch. She studied my face for a long moment before speaking. "You know, don't you?"

The words left me breathless. "Yes."

She sighed deeply. "Rob and I have been getting calls every week."

"From developers?"

"From Shane first," she said. "Then from men we've never met."

Rob stepped out behind her, a limp in his gait. "They keep telling us this land isn't worth much," he said. "That we should sell before the taxes rise."

"Same thing they told Dee," Loretta added.

"And you didn't believe them?"

Loretta's eyes sharpened. "Honey, I've lived long enough to know when someone's trying to steal something."

By afternoon, we were sitting in Dee's diner.

Dee poured coffee for all of us. Her hands trembled slightly. "They came to me last week," she said.

"Developers?" I asked.

She nodded and patted her beehive. "Offered to buy the diner."

"For how much?"

She named the number.

Loretta snorted. "That land's worth almost triple that amount."

Dee looked tired. "They told me I should sell before it's taken."

My stomach turned. "Taken? I don't get it. What does that mean?"

"Eminent domain," Rob said grimly. "Or zoning changes."

We all fell silent.

I stared at the lukewarm coffee in front of me. A jumble of thoughts swirled through my mind. Michael's note. The barn ledgers. The life insurance withdrawal. Gabe's voice echoing in my head. *There's no place like Home.*

I lifted my head. "No."

Everyone stared at me.

"They think they can scare us," I said slowly. "They think we'll sell cheap and disappear."

Loretta's eyes gleamed. "What're you suggesting?"

I stood and gathered my purse. "We fight."

Dee raised an eyebrow. "How, hon?" she asked as she stood and adjusted her apron. "It feels like I've exhausted every avenue I know, and you know me, I sure ain't one to be bullied around, but this one's got me."

I thought of Owen. Of the ledgers. Of Destiny, seeing ghosts in the barn. Of the pearl in my jewelry box. "This town has secrets," I said. "And Shane has been hiding them."

Rob stood and leaned forward to help his wife to her feet. "And what happens now?"

"We start telling the truth," I said.

Dee nodded and grabbed the empty coffee pot like it was a sword. "That's dang straight. I'm tired of being sick and tired. Those bullies can kiss my grits."

We laughed as we huddled beside the exit to say our goodbyes and plan our next move. Outside, the wind whistled through the trees, causing the limbs to bend and sway as if giving us a hero's send-off.

As I started my car and began my drive home, I realized something.

This town didn't just belong to Shane.

It belonged to the people who refused to leave it.

And I wasn't leaving.

Not without a fight.

Chapter 40

Gabe

Gabe sat alone in his truck outside the diner long after the neon OPEN sign had gone dark.

The ledger pages lay on the passenger seat.

Numbers. Names. Acres.

He had seen the handwriting before—his father's blocky script. Pops had always kept records that way, neat and square, like a man who believed if you wrote something down clean enough, it became truth.

But Gabe now knew those numbers weren't the truth.

He ran a hand through his hair and leaned back against the seat.

Investment, his father had called it. Opportunity. Like an idiot, Gabe had believed him.

His father had come to him after Michael died, voice heavy with sympathy and wisdom.

"Your brother would've wanted that money to grow. For Ebony. For the kids."

So, Gabe had signed the papers.

Transferred part of Michael's life insurance into a development fund Shane controlled.

He had told himself he was helping the family.

Helping Ebony.

Helping the town.

Now the ledger said something different. Now the ledger said he had helped steal their land. Gabe slammed his palm against the steering wheel. "Dang it." The sound echoed through the empty parking lot. He picked up the ledger again. The names glared back at him. Wilson. Dee Carter. Ebony McMullen. And beside each one—A price. Cheap. Criminally cheap.

He swallowed hard as he put his truck in drive and made his way to Ebony's house. Pops isn't just selling land. He's clearing the town.

He pulled onto Morning Glory Road as Ebony's porch light flickered.

Gabe stared at it for a long time before finally climbing out of the truck.

The gravel crunched under his boots as he crossed the yard. He knocked once. The door opened almost immediately.

Ebony stood there in socks and a sweater, arms folded.

"I see you got my message," she said.

Gabe nodded. "Eb, I'm so sorry. I thought it was an investment," he said quietly.

Her eyes didn't soften. "That's what people say when they realize they've been used."

"I didn't know Pops was targeting your house," Gabe said. "Or the Wilsons. Or Dee."

"But you signed the papers."

Gabe looked at the floor. "Yeah."

"Come inside," Ebony said, moving aside so he could enter.

He stepped inside and placed the ledger on the coffee table. "I'm done helping him," he said.

Ebony studied him carefully. "You're his son. You talked all this stuff about being at odds with your father. But it's clear that the apple doesn't fall far from the tree."

"Michael was my brother. I would never do anything to harm him or his family. I really thought what I was doing was going to work out for all of us and that—"

"Just stop." Her expression darkened. "You didn't seem to remember that when you stole money from his life insurance policy. The money we needed. How could you? I thought we were friends."

"It's not what you think." He pushed the ledger toward her. "There's so much more to this," he said. "Pops didn't just pressure people to sell. He set up shell buyers, so it looks like normal purchases."

"I don't get it." Ebony flipped through the pages. "These are developers?"

He nodded. "Waiting for the land to be cleared."

She exhaled slowly. "If what you're saying is true, then you need to be the one to help us expose it."

"We need proof—"

"Hi, Uncle Gabe, where's Kid?" From the hallway, Destiny's voice floated in.

Both adults turned as the child waved.

"He couldn't come this time, Squirt."

Destiny walked to her uncle and hugged his leg. "Don't worry, you can bring him next time." She rubbed her eyes. "The lady says you already have proof."

"What lady?"

Destiny stood with Lady B tucked under her arm. Her wide eyes were fixed on Ebony. "The pretty lady," she said softly.

Chapter 41

Ebony

Ebony's stomach tightened. "The one with the pearls?"

Destiny nodded, clutching Lady B beneath her chin. "She says the secret is inside the pearl."

The words hung in the room like a draft slipping under a closed door.

Ebony looked from Destiny to Gabe, then to the ledger on the table. Her pulse quickened. Nothing about the night felt ordinary anymore—the barn, the ledgers, Michael's warning. Nothing.

"Show us," Ebony said softly.

Minutes later, the cool night air wrapped around them as they crossed the yard.

The barn loomed at the edge of the property, its tall frame dark against the moonlit sky. The lantern Owen carried cast long, swinging shadows as he pushed the door open.

The hinges groaned.

Inside, the smell of wood, hay, and old earth rose to meet them.

Owen set the lantern on a crate near the loft ladder.

"You brought Uncle Gabe?" he asked cautiously. His eyes shifted toward his uncle, hard and guarded. "Why?"

Gabe stepped into the lantern light.

"He's the one we should be calling the police on," Owen added, his jaw tight.

"I'm on your side now," Gabe said.

Owen crossed his arms but didn't answer.

Ebony felt the tension ripple through the room like wind across water. For a moment, she thought Owen might push further, but he stayed quiet.

Destiny wandered slowly across the barn floor, her slippers whispering through scattered straw. "She's here," she whispered.

Ebony followed her gaze instinctively, though she saw nothing except the long wooden wall and the old tack cabinet in the corner.

"Who's here?" Scotty's voice cut through the barn.

Everyone turned.

Scotty stood in the doorway, barefoot, his hair sticking up like he'd rolled straight out of bed. "I woke up, and the house was empty," he said. "What are you all doing out here?" Then he noticed Gabe. His eyebrows shot up. "Uncle Gabe?"

Gabe lifted a hand in a half-wave. "Hey, kid."

Scotty looked from Gabe to the ledgers in Owen's hands, then to Destiny wandering deeper into the barn like she belonged there. "Okay," he muttered. "What did I miss?"

"A lot," Owen said quietly.

Scotty rubbed the back of his neck and stepped fully inside, letting the barn door swing shut behind him.

The lantern flickered.

Destiny stopped walking. She raised one small finger and pointed toward the far wall. "There," she said softly.

Ebony followed the direction of her hand.

The old tack cabinet stood where it always had, its wood dark with age and its latch rusted from years of neglect.

Destiny took another small step toward it. "She's standing right there."

A chill slid through Ebony's spine.

Scotty glanced around uneasily. "Desi, who's standing there?"

"The lady," Destiny said.

"The one with the pearls?" Owen asked.

Destiny nodded.

Ebony slipped her arm around her daughter's shoulders.

Behind them, Gabe stepped closer to the cabinet. "You sure about this?" he asked quietly.

Destiny looked up at him with complete certainty. "She said you'd find it tonight."

Owen climbed the loft ladder and lifted the lantern higher, throwing more light across the cabinet. "Locked," he said.

Gabe walked forward slowly. "Then let's see what the barn's been keeping from us."

The wood creaked softly overhead, the sound echoing through the beams like a breath long held. And Ebony couldn't shake the feeling that something—someone—had been waiting a very long time for them to open that door.

Ebony knelt beside Destiny.

"Who?"

"The lady. "Destiny pointed toward the far wall. "There."

Gabe frowned. "That's just an old tack cabinet."

Destiny shook her head. "She's standing by it."

Owen climbed the ladder and shone the lantern toward the cabinet.

Locked," he said.

Gabe stepped forward. "Let me try, son." One solid hit from a pry bar popped the rusted latch. The door creaked open.

Inside sat a small wooden box.

Dust coated the lid.

Ebony's pulse quickened. She opened it slowly.

Inside—

Letters.

Old photographs.

And a folded piece of cloth wrapped around something hard.

Ebony unwrapped it.

The large pearl rolled gently into her palm. A pearl similar to the one Mrs. Loretta had given her months ago. Only much bigger.

"The lady said it opens," Destiny whispered.

Ebony frowned. "Pearls don't open, Princess."

Gabe leaned closer. "Let me see." He turned the pearl in the lantern light.

Then he saw it. A faint seam. "Holy—"

He twisted carefully.

The pearl split in two.

Inside was a tiny, rolled strip of paper.

Owen leaned forward.

"Is that—"

Ebony unrolled it slowly.

A note. Old but preserved.

"The deed is in the clasp." Her breath caught as she read the words aloud.

"What's a clasp?" Owen asked.

"It's a part of a necklace that looks like a decorative gold bead or cylinder. One end slides or unscrews and keeps the—"

"Wait." Owen rummaged through the box, finding what he was searching for, and held it up. "Is this it?" he asked as he rotated the tarnished, long, slender piece of silver.

Ebony nodded. "Check to see if anything is in there."

Owen shook the clasp several times until a tediously rolled piece of paper slipped out from it into his hand. He unrolled it carefully and squinted in the dim light. "It looks like it's a property deed, signed many years ago."

Ebony leaned over to read the worn scrap of paper Owen had spread out before them. Though ragged, it was perfectly intact. The landowner's name made her step back. "Shane McMullen's great-grandmother," she whispered. Ebony scanned the document again.

Below the signature—

Another name. Mrs. Loretta's family name. And written in careful ink:

Joint ownership of the barn property and surrounding acres. Ebony looked up slowly. "That means—"

"Pops never owned this land outright," Gabe finished. "He searched all over for that paperwork and could never find it. He had some shady lawyer draft up fake documents years ago…"

Owen's eyes widened. "The developers can't buy what he doesn't legally control."

Destiny smiled and hugged her ladybug pillow. "The lady said you'd find it."

Ebony folded the document carefully. For the first time since Michael died, real hope bloomed in her heart. The kind of God-given hope that no one and nothing could ever steal.

They didn't just have suspicion.

They had proof.

And somewhere in the dark beams above them, the barn creaked softly— as if history itself had just exhaled and all the colors of Home had painted the perfect picture.

My Dearest Ebony,

From the moment I met you, I knew I'd found the one my soul longed for. You are my heart and my best friend. The love of my life. No one has ever belonged to someone like I belong to you.

Owen, Scotty, and our sweet Destiny — together we've built a home filled with more love than I'd ever dreamed possible. I've always thought I was the luckiest man alive.

If you're reading this, it means I'm gone now. I can't imagine leaving this world, this family. And yet, love, if that day has truly come, you have to promise me something. You have to keep your hope in God.

Faith is the prayer I pray as I drift into my last sleep, the hope I have for you and the kids as I leave this world. Hold on to it with all you have, Eb. No matter what happens, no matter where your path leads, never give up on Him.

God is with you when you're sure and when you doubt. When you're strong and when you're breaking. He's beside you when you're calm and when you're angry, when there are answers and when there are none. And if the cancer takes me, He will hold you close and hold our children even closer.

No matter what, God will be your hope. Let that hope be the song you sing our babies to sleep. Let it be your strength when you stand tall and your anchor when you fall to your knees.

♡ Michael

A Note from Edwina Perkins

Some people believe recipes are just instructions—a way to measure flour or stir a pot. But in my family, recipes were always more than that. They were memories passed down quietly, the way stories travel from one generation to the next.

A pie crust taught by a grandmother.

A skillet of chicken that fed a house full of people after a long day.

Warm milk at night when the world felt uncertain.

In the South, food carries history. It holds the laughter, the sorrow, the prayers, and the small moments that make a house feel like home.

The recipes in these pages are the kind that live in worn notebooks and in the hands of people who cook more by heart than by measurement. They are simple, honest, and meant to be shared.

If you make one of these dishes, I hope it brings the same warmth to your kitchen that it once brought to mine.

And remember—the best meals are never just about what's on the table.

They're about the people gathered around it.

With love,

Edwina Perkins

A Taste of Home: Stories & Recipes from the Southern Kitchen

Food carries memory. In the South, a recipe is rarely just a recipe. It is a story passed from one pair of hands to another — from grandmothers to daughters, from church kitchens to family tables. These dishes are the kind that fill a house with warmth, the kind that remind us that even in difficult seasons, there is always comfort waiting at the table.

Sweet Potato Fried Pies:

The kitchen always smelled like cinnamon when sweet potatoes were baking. My grandmother said sweet potatoes were a gift from the earth itself — humble, sturdy, and able to feed a family through lean times.

When the pies were finished frying, she would line them up on brown paper bags to cool. We, children, would circle the table like little hawks waiting for our turn.

She would pretend not to notice us sneaking closer and say, "Now don't burn your mouth. Good things are worth waiting for."

And of course, we never waited.

Sweet Potato Fried Pies Recipe:

These small hand pies were common in Southern kitchens because they traveled well and could be eaten warm or cold. Sweet potato filling makes them rich, comforting, and deeply Southern.

Ingredients:

For the Dough:

- 2 cups all-purpose flour
- 1 teaspoon salt
- ½ cup cold butter or shortening
- ½ cup cold water

For the Filling

- 2 cups mashed cooked sweet potatoes
- ½ cup brown sugar
- 1 teaspoon cinnamon
- ½ teaspoon nutmeg
- 1 teaspoon vanilla extract
- 2 tablespoons butter
- pinch of salt

For Frying

- vegetable oil

Instructions:

1. In a bowl mix flour and salt. Cut in butter until crumbly.
2. Add cold water slowly until dough forms. Wrap and chill 30 minutes.
3. Mix sweet potatoes, brown sugar, cinnamon, nutmeg, vanilla, butter, and salt.
4. Roll dough thin and cut into circles.
5. Place a spoonful of filling on one side and fold over to make a half-moon.
6. Seal edges with a fork.
7. Fry in hot oil until golden brown.
8. Drain on paper towels and serve warm.

Apple Fried Pies:

Apple pies were the kind you could carry with you — wrapped in a napkin and slipped into a coat pocket before heading out the door.

Farmers took them to the fields. Children carried them to school. Travelers packed them for the road.

My aunt used to say a good apple pie could make a long journey feel shorter. Something about warm fruit and flaky crust reminds you that somewhere, someone cared enough to cook for you.

Apple Fried Pies Recipe:

Apple fried pies were often sold at roadside stands and church gatherings across the South.

Ingredients:

For the Dough:

- 2 cups flour
- ½ teaspoon salt
- ½ cup butter or shortening
- ½ cup cold water

For the Filling:

- 2 cups diced apples
- ½ cup sugar
- 1 teaspoon cinnamon
- 1 tablespoon lemon juice
- 2 tablespoons butter
- 1 tablespoon cornstarch

Instructions:

1. Prepare the dough the same way as the sweet potato pies.
2. Cook apples, sugar, cinnamon, lemon juice, butter, and cornstarch in a saucepan until soft and thickened.
3. Roll the dough and cut circles.
4. Add the apple filling and fold into half-moons.
5. Seal edges with a fork.
6. Fry until golden brown.
7. Dust with powdered sugar if desired.

Vanilla Hot Chocolate (aka White Chocolate, Destiny's favorite):

Not every comfort drink in the South needed chocolate. Some nights, all you needed was warm milk sweetened with brown sugar and a whisper of cinnamon.

My mother made this when the house was quiet, and the world felt a little heavy. She would warm the milk slowly on the stove and stir it with a wooden spoon as if it were something sacred.

"Drink this," she'd say, handing me the mug.

"It settles the soul."

And somehow, it always did.

Vanilla Hot Chocolate Recipe:

This comforting drink is more like sweet, spiced milk, often served on cold nights or before bed.

Ingredients:

- 2 cups whole milk
- 2 tablespoons brown sugar
- 1 teaspoon vanilla extract
- ¼ teaspoon cinnamon
- pinch of salt

Instructions:

1. Warm milk in a saucepan over medium heat (do not boil).
2. Stir in brown sugar, cinnamon, and salt.
3. Remove from heat and add vanilla.

4. Whisk until slightly frothy.

5. Serve warm.

Old-Fashioned Vanilla/Chocolate Milkshake:

Milkshakes meant summer. Hot pavement, cicadas singing in the trees, and the slow whir of a blender in the kitchen.

We didn't need fancy flavors. Vanilla was enough. Thick, cold, and sweet—the kind you had to sip slowly because the straw kept getting stuck.

Sometimes the simplest things become the memories that stay with us the longest.

Old-Fashioned Vanilla/ Chocolate Milkshake Recipe:

A simple Southern treat perfect after supper or on a hot afternoon.

Ingredients:

- 2 cups vanilla OR chocolate ice cream
- 1 cup cold milk
- 1 teaspoon vanilla extract
- whipped cream (optional)
- Maraschino cherries

Instructions:

1. Place ice cream, milk, and vanilla extract in a blender.
2. Blend until thick and creamy.
3. Pour into a tall glass.

4. Top with whipped cream if desired.

5. Add a maraschino cherry on top.

Southern Garlic Chicken:

Every Southern kitchen has a dish that means home. For many families, that dish is chicken cooking in a skillet.

The smell of garlic and butter drifting through the house meant dinner was close. It meant someone cared enough to gather everyone around the table.

In the South, meals aren't just about eating. They're about pausing long enough to remember that we belong to one another.

Southern Garlic Chicken Recipe:

This simple garlic chicken is flavorful, buttery, and perfect served with rice, biscuits, or greens

Ingredients:

- 4 chicken thighs or breasts
- 4 cloves garlic, minced
- 3 tablespoons butter
- 1 tablespoon olive oil
- 1 teaspoon paprika
- 1 teaspoon salt
- ½ teaspoon black pepper
- ½ teaspoon thyme
- ½ cup chicken broth

Instructions:

1. Season chicken with salt, pepper, paprika, and thyme.
2. Heat oil and butter in a skillet over medium heat.
3. Brown chicken on both sides until golden.
4. Add garlic and cook for about 30 seconds.
5. Pour in chicken broth.
6. Cover and simmer for 15–20 minutes, until the chicken is cooked through.
7. Spoon garlic sauce over the chicken before serving.

Fresh Lemonade:

The weather in Home could wrap around you like a warm quilt. The kind of heat that made the cicadas sing louder and the dust rise slowly from the dirt road on Morning Glory Road.

On those afternoons, Ebony would set a pitcher of lemonade on the porch table before the children even thought to ask for it. The lemons were bright and sharp against the wooden cutting board, their scent filling the kitchen with something clean and hopeful.

Destiny liked to help squeeze them, though she always made a face at the sourness. The boys would hover nearby, pretending they weren't waiting for the first glass.

There was something about lemonade in the South. It wasn't just a drink. It was an invitation to slow down. To sit. To talk. To remember.

And sometimes, on quiet afternoons, Ebony would watch the sun dip toward the trees and think that maybe healing came the same way lemonade did—a little sweet, a little tart, and best when shared.

Fresh Southern Lemonade Recipe:

Ingredients:

- 1 cup freshly squeezed lemon juice (about 4–6 lemons)
- ¾ cup sugar
- 4 cups cold water
- Ice
- Lemon slices for garnish (optional)

Instructions:

1. In a small saucepan, combine ¾ cup sugar and 1 cup water.
2. Heat over medium heat until the sugar dissolves completely to create a simple syrup.
3. Remove from heat and allow to cool.
4. In a large pitcher, combine the fresh lemon juice, simple syrup, and remaining 3 cups cold water.
5. Stir well.
6. Serve over ice and garnish with lemon slices if desired.

Tip: For an extra Southern touch, add a few sprigs of fresh mint.

Chocolate Chip Cookies:

The smell of baking cookies could make a house feel like home faster than almost anything else.

Ebony didn't bake them often—life had been too busy for that—but every once in a while, usually on a rainy afternoon, she would pull out the mixing bowl her grandmother once used.

The children would know what was coming the moment the butter softened on the counter.

Flour would dust the air.

Brown sugar would spill over the measuring cup.

And someone—usually the youngest—would sneak a handful of chocolate chips before they ever reached the dough.

When the cookies finally came out of the oven, golden at the edges and soft in the center, the whole kitchen smelled like warmth and forgiveness.

Ebony believed baking cookies was a little like building a family.

It took patience.

A few sweet ingredients.

And a willingness to share the last one on the plate.

Classic Chocolate Chip Cookies Recipe:

Ingredients:

- 1 cup butter, softened
- ¾ cup brown sugar
- ¾ cup white sugar
- 2 eggs
- 2 teaspoons vanilla extract
- 2 ¼ cups all-purpose flour
- 1 teaspoon baking soda

- ½ teaspoon salt

- 2 cups chocolate chips

Instructions:

1. Preheat oven to 350°F.
2. In a large bowl, cream together butter, brown sugar, and white sugar until light and fluffy.
3. Beat in the eggs one at a time, then stir in the vanilla extract.
4. In another bowl, mix flour, baking soda, and salt.
5. Gradually add the dry ingredients to the wet mixture.
6. Stir in the chocolate chips.
7. Drop spoonfuls of dough onto a lined baking sheet.
8. Bake for 9–11 minutes, until the edges are golden.
9. Let cool slightly before serving.

Tip: For a soft, bakery-style cookie, chill the dough 30 minutes before baking.

The Colors of Home:
Book Club Discussion Guide

About the Book:

The Colors of Home follows Ebony, a widow raising three children, as she returns to her small Southern hometown. Confronted with family secrets, a mysterious heirloom pearl, and unresolved past conflicts, Ebony embarks on a journey that explores themes of family, resilience, identity, and the true meaning of home.

This guide is designed to facilitate thoughtful discussions about character motivations, historical and cultural context, symbolism, and the story's emotional impact.

Historical Context: Heirlooms and Hidden Legacies:

In the American South, it was not uncommon for enslaved women to receive jewelry from slave owners, particularly men who fathered children with them. While these gifts could appear as tokens of affection, they sometimes carried deeper significance: jewelry could hide important documents, freedom papers, or evidence of inheritance or land bequeathed to enslaved families.

These small objects became powerful tools for survival, preservation, and legacy. They allowed families to pass down history, claim rights, and protect future generations—even in the face of oppression.

In *The Colors of Home*, the heirloom pearl Ebony discovers echoes this history. It is not just a beautiful object; it is a vessel of memory, resilience, and the enduring fight for family legacy.

Themes to Explore:

1. **Family & Legacy**

   - How do family secrets shape Ebony's present?

   - How do generational traumas or traditions influence the behavior of different characters?

   - How do Ebony's children reflect or challenge family history?

   - How does the heirloom necklace symbolize legacy, history, and the survival of family memory?

2. **Home & Belonging**

   - How does the novel define "home"? Is it physical, emotional, or both?

   - Compare Ebony's childhood home and the house she returns to—how do they influence her sense of belonging?

3. **Resilience & Survival**

   - How does Ebony navigate grief and loss?

   - How do historical realities of survival, like hiding documents or preserving family legacy, influence her journey?

4. **Secrets & Truth**

   - How do secrets protect or harm individuals?

- How does the necklace serve as a symbol of hidden histories and resilience?

5. **Faith & Morality (if applicable)**

   - How does spirituality influence decisions or perspectives in the story?
   - Are there moments when faith shapes Ebony's resilience?

Character Discussion Guide:

Ebony

- How does she change from the beginning to the end of the novel?
- What motivates her decisions regarding her children, her home, and the heirloom?
- How does she balance past trauma with present challenges?

Shane / Family Elders

- How do the grandfather or other elder figures impact the family dynamics?
- How do their choices create tension or conflict in Ebony's life?
- Children
- How do the children reflect themes of innocence, legacy, or hope?
- How does Ebony's parenting shape their understanding of family and identity?

Supporting Characters

- Which secondary characters stood out and why?
- Do any characters serve as mirrors or contrasts to Ebony?

Chapter & Plot Discussion Prompts:

Opening Chapters:

- How is Ebony introduced?
- What immediate challenges does she face, and how does this set the tone for the novel?
- How does the setting of the Southern town contribute to the story?

Middle Chapters:

- Discuss the discovery of the heirloom and family secrets. How do these moments change Ebony's perspective?
- How do the town's history and attitudes toward Ebony reflect broader social or cultural themes?
- How does the historical context of jewelry, hidden documents, and legacy deepen the meaning of the heirloom?

Ending Chapters:

- How does the resolution reconcile past conflicts?
- Are all questions answered, or are some left open? How does this affect your reading experience?
- What does Ebony ultimately learn about herself and her family?

Quotes for Discussion:

1. "Some houses keep secrets, and some memories refuse to die quietly."
2. What does this quote suggest about the novel's central conflict?

3. "Sometimes the truest history of a family isn't written in records at all—it's remembered in the food that brings us back to one another."

4. How does this connect to the Southern recipes and traditions described in the book?

5. "The place that broke you can be the very place that holds the power to heal you."

6. How does this reflect Ebony's journey?

7. "A small object can hold the weight of generations."

8. How does the heirloom necklace illustrate this idea?

Reflection Questions:

1. How do objects (like the heirloom necklace) serve as symbols in the story?

2. How does the novel portray the tension between past and present?

3. How do secrets and hidden histories influence relationships across generations?

4. How does the historical context of slavery and hidden legacy influence your understanding of the story?

5. Did you identify with Ebony or any other character? Why?

6. How does the Southern setting influence the story? Could the story take place elsewhere?

Activities for Book Club Meetings:

1. Recipe Connection: Prepare a Southern recipe from the novel (Sweet Potato Fried Pies or Vanilla Cinnamon Hot Milk) and discuss the story as you share it.

2. Family Heirloom Discussion: Ask members to bring a meaningful family object and share its story. How does it carry memory or history like the heirloom in the novel?

3. Character Journals: Write a short journal entry from Ebony's perspective at a pivotal moment. How does she feel? What is she thinking but not saying?

4. Setting Visualization: Draw or describe the Southern town and Ebony's home. How does the setting reflect the characters' emotional landscapes?

5. Story Continuation: Imagine a scene that happens after the book ends. How do the characters continue to navigate their lives and relationships?

Optional Book Club Activity Section:

1. Create a "Colors of Home" Playlist: Build a playlist of songs that reflect the novel's themes of home, family, and resilience. Play it while discussing key chapters.

2. Map the Town: Have members draw a map of the Southern town based on descriptions in the book. Mark significant locations like Ebony's house, schools, or places tied to family history.

3. Recipe Challenge: Assign each member a Southern recipe from the novel to prepare before the next meeting. Share photos and taste impressions online or in person.

4. Legacy Letters: Write a letter to a family member (real or fictional) reflecting on what "home" means to you. Share with the group if comfortable.

5. The Heirloom Game: Bring an object or small token that represents your family story. Discuss why it matters, connecting it to the heirloom's significance in the book.

6. Historical Reflection Activity: Research how enslaved families used jewelry or other small objects to preserve legacy, freedom papers, or inheritance. Discuss how this history deepens the heirloom's meaning in Ebony's story.

Closing Reflection for the Group:

The Colors of Home reminds us that the stories we inherit, the objects we treasure, and the meals we share all carry history, identity, and love. Discussing these themes as a group allows readers to reflect on their own families, traditions, and the meaning of home.

Final Question:

- If you could give Ebony one piece of advice or encouragement at the end of the story, what would it be?

Edwina Perkins is the co-director of Blue Ridge Mountains Christian Writers Conference. She is the coordinator for Mentoring Moments and the manager for Sensitivity Between the Lines, both with Blue Ridge Mountains Christian Writers Conference. Edwina is the managing editor for Harambee Press. As a longtime member of Word Weavers International, she now serves on the advisory board. She has served as the Emerging Leader Coordinator with ECPA (Evangelical Christian Publishing Association).

Edwina is an award-winning writer, experienced teacher, speaker, freelance editor, and authenticity/sensitivity consultant, and has been published in numerous publications.

Edwina has a passion for seeing ethnic writers represented well in the publishing industry, and she enjoys speaking to audiences about this opportunity. She is also passionate about coaching and mentoring writers.

9 781970 354171